I0596663

CRUDDY BUDDIES

Dion C. Williams aka D. Will

Cruddy Buddies

"Cruddy Buddies" Act I & Act II

By: Dion C. Williams aka D. Will

Cover Designed By: Jazzy Kitty Publishing

Cover images: www.photobucket.com, www.wbaltv.com

Logo Designs By: Andre M. Saunders

Editor: Anelda L. Attaway

ACKNOWLEDGMENTS

First and foremost all praises due to Allah (God). He and he alone is the reason I am blessed with and able to share with the readers and my fans, the vision known as my work.

I would like to thank also the two greatest forces in my life; Mr. John R. Williams (my Dad) and Mrs. Sheila J. Williams (my Mother) because without their patience, perseverance, and love, who knows where I would be. Mom and Dad, you continued to believe in me when there was nothing left and I cannot thank you or express enough love for that. I LOVE YOU!!!

I want to thank the other powerful force in my life, my backbone, my rock, my little ball of courage, and my strength; Ms. Kia C. Williams (my sister). I don't know where to start; I can never thank you or apologize enough. You kept me together when I fell apart. Again I thank you and I love you!!

To all my children and other special members of my Clan I do this for and with you. I Love You!!

To Simmeon Anderson for putting me on to the game.

And Last but not least, Anelda Attaway and the Jazzy Kitty Publishing Staff. Thank you for taking a chance. I promise to not let you down.

TABLE OF CONTENTS/ACT I

TABLE OF CONTENTS/ACT II

INTRODUCTION

The definition of Cruddy Buddy is it an informal noun which means a good friend that you can do dirt with, a partner in crime...

"What's this all about?" asked a frightened Omar.

"I talk...you listen!" snapped Cash, "where is the Money and the Shit?"

"I don't know what you mean?" said Omar.

"FO, show Omar what we mean please."

FO raised the barrel of his all black AR-15 and shot the first guard in his face, blowing bits of his skull and brain matter all over the floor and walls.

Next he shot guard number two center mass, rupturing his diaphragm causing him to bleed internally and suffocate.

The female crack fiend was next. He emptied the rest of the clip into her face and chest as he began to smile as Omar flinched.

"Now, where is the Money and the Shit!" asked Cash.

"In the basement!" yelled Omar, "please don't kill me please!"

CHAPTER 1

Business as Usual

"Oh yes! Yes! Right there Daddy! Don't stop! Ooh, don't stop! I'm Cumming!" screamed Tanika, "please Daddy don't stop!"

Tanika's vocal display had Cash feeling like he was the Shit when it came to gorilla Fucking these hood rat Bitches. Not to mention the fact that the Percocets and Ciroc in his system had him feeling like he couldn't stop. Suddenly, his work phone started playing the ring tone of Brown Paper Bags by DJ Khalid. He immediately, pulled out of the pussy and answered the phone to the dismay of Tanika.

"Whas good?" he answered.

The voice on the other end of the phone said, "Are you available?"

Cash answered "yes" and began to record the needed information. After writing down the information, he gave the caller an account number and said that he expected half of his fee of $25,000 to be transferred within the hour. The rest upon completion of the job. After this, he hung up and turned his attention back to Tanika.

"What the Fuck, you all in my grill for? You mad at me or something?" he asked.

"I asked you not to stop Cash!" she said angrily.

"Look here you hood rat bitch! That was money and money is always over bitches you dig? So you either, shut up and put this dick in your mouth or get up and get the Fuck out."

"Cash you make me sick," she said while at the same time grabbing his dick and deep throating it.

As Cash was receiving the good head piece he grabbed his iPhone and preceded to text his partner FO Pound, and alerts him to the new job and let him know to be ready to move by 1am. He then dropped the phone right before he came all in Tanika's throat.

After dropping Tanika off at her crib Cash picked up FO and placed a call to his gun connect and main man Mello. He placed an order with Mello for 2 Heckler and Koch HP-Assault Rifles, 2 Smith and Wesson Glocks, 40 Caliber handguns, extra ammo, and 2 stage 3 body armor bullet proof vest. Mello said he would have everything ready and waiting for Cash to pick-up within the hour. 60 minutes later!

Upon reaching Mello's spot downtown in the warehouse district, Cash and FO were met and frisked at the door by Mello's security team. Once they were relieved of their weapons they were checked for entry.

"I better get my 45 back you Bitch ass Nigga or else I'm going to kill your family and Fuck your grandma in her ass Raw!" said FO to the security dude.

"It's cool FO," said Cash, before there could be a confrontation, "we good, let's go dawg."

"Aright but, I still don't like his fake Deebo looking ass," said FO while mean mugging the security dude.

As they walked inside Cash laughed and said, "He do, look like a broke ass body builder."

"Yo Mello! Whas good, my Nigga?" asked Cash and FO while exchanging dap with the gun man.

"Shit! But, I see FO still giving my security team the blues every chance he gets."

"Ain't Shit changed," said FO.

"I can't make it easy on them, they gotta earn their money," he said and they all laughed at that.

"Oh yeah Cash, tell your Little Brother 40 he still owe me $200 for that Tech-9 he bought last week."

"No sweat Mello, I got him covered," said Cash, "here is $4700 instead of the $4500."

"You can't keep saving his lil ass out, you heard me?" said Mello.

"Man Shawty crazy like his Big Bro," said FO.

"Now, I know FO ain't just call me crazy! If that ain't the pot calling the kettle black! Anyway, Mello, we gotta dip! Duty calls I'll holla when we need you dawg," said Cash.

Then with that FO and Cash loaded up and headed towards D.C., because there was an unfinished job and money to be made.

CHAPTER 2

Show Time

After loading up and strapping on the body armor they posted up across the street from the Ramada Inn at the end of Route 50 in D.C. They then began to go over the plan.

"This is the deal FO," said Cash. Our mark is this 2 bit dealer named Frog. Frog is meeting with a D.C. connect to cop a couple birds to take back to Baltimore and flood the block with. Our job is to make sure he doesn't return. Whatever else we find inside that room is ours, a come up ya dig?"

"I feel that," said FO.

"What rooms they in Cash?"

"223 and 225, the rooms adjoin so this is what we gonna do, you take the stairs at this end of the building and I'll take the ones' at the opposite end. Then we walk down and hit both rooms at the same time, mark everything and everybody, clean up and bounce out! You know how we do it my Nigga, No Witnesses!"

"Yeah No Witnesses," said FO and with that they pulled the limo-tinted Chevy Impala into the parking lot.

They waited in the car until Frog and his connect arrived and checked in before they made their moves. The 1st thing they did was case the joint and made sure there were no surprises, which there weren't. Then they got out and headed toward the stairs. They stopped in the stairwells and masked up. 5 minutes later they were locked, cocked, and loaded. They gave each other the silent signal and kicked both doors in the same time. Frogs room was empty because everyone was in the connects room. They had the element of surprise so Frog and The Plug were Fucked.

"What the Fuck is this Hernando?" asked Frog.

"You tell me Homes," said the connect.

"Both of y'all Shut the Fuck Up and you just might live," lied FO.

Frog looked like he had just Shit a brick. Hernando's bodyguards kept inching and moving around so Cash put a 40 caliber hollow tip in each of their faces blowing bone and brain matter all over the walls behind them.

Next Cash asked Frog, "Where is the Money?"

Frog promptly gave it up after witnessing the execution of the guards.

"Now it's your turn Poppi, where is the Shit?" asked FO.

Hernando trying to work things out said, "Fellas can't we come to an agreement here? I'll give you 10 of the 30 bricks I have and you can keep his $600,000 because, I need 2 men of your caliber to work for me."

Cash responded by shooting Hernando in both legs, "NOW, one more time! Where is the Shit?"

Hernando fearing for his life gave up the keys to a black cherry 2010 Range Rover Port and said, "In the parking lot, all 30 are in the back."

After a search of the room FO relieved them both of their cell phones, jewelry, and cash.

FO said, "Now, for the last order of business. Hey Frog! You know your boss Angel?"

Frog replied, "Yes," with glimmer of hope in his eyes. "What about him?"

Cash and FO raised the HP5's and said at the same time... "He said he'll see you in Hell."

Then they both emptied the assault rifles into Frog and Hernando killing them both instantly. They quickly cleaned up, loaded the vehicles and left the hotel unseen but not unheard.

CHAPTER 3

Once Again it's On

Two weeks later, and a half a mil richer C-4 (Cash & FO) was ready to lay back and relax a little. Cash and FO sat in the living room of FO's mother, Momma Jefferies home on a Sunday afternoon. They both were eagerly awaiting her to finish cooking dinner.

"Oooooh weeee! That smell so good Momma, what you cooking?" asked FO.

"Daniel I'm cooking roast beef, collard greens, baked chicken, mashed potatoes, gravy, and carrot cake for dessert why!!?"

"Cuz we starving Momma."

"Well if y'all would stop smoking them ole funny ass cigarettes you'll wouldn't have the munchies," said Mrs. Jefferies.

"I plead the fifth," said Cash.

"I bet you do Calvin," said Momma Jefferies.

"Boy I sure miss your momma, seems like only yesterday my best friend was right here with me."

"Yes, Ma'am, I miss her too, Momma Jefferies."

"When you gonna settle down and meet you a nice girl and leave them hood rats in the hood? You and Daniel need to stop thinking with y'all little heads, life don't last forever you know!"

"Yes Ma'am," they both answered.

After dinner and 2 more blunts it was time to go to work again. This job was a simple stash house robbery in East Baltimore. Some dudes had tried to cut in on an established block off of Glover Street and then Glover Street Boys wasn't having that. So a call was made, C-4 was paid and now it was time for the Mac's to be sprayed. Cash dialed Mello from his iPhone while sitting in the passenger seat of FO's Lexus LS460.

"Yo!" answered Mello.

"I'm coming thru my Nigg, Big Mac's and Fries!"

"Ok done deal Baby Boy and Oh yeah, 40 is into me for $450 this time!"

"No prob see you in the Drive Thru," said Cash and then hung up.

FO asked, "Sure we good?"

"Yeah we good but let me call my Lil Brother and see what his problem is."

"What, he owe Mello again?"

"Yeah."

"That Lil Nigga really is crazy," laughed FO. Cash speed dialed the number for his Lil Brother 40 Cal.

"Hello," said Cash.

"What up Big Bro whats good?" asked Cal.

"You tell me you Lil Shit, why do I, keep having to pay your bill with Mello? I know you ain't broke, I just gave you 5 chickens to hatch."

"Nah I ain't broke, he just charge too much for them shirts Cash!"

"How he charge too much for new joints and whatever else we need? Cal stop being petty! Anyway I got a job for you."

"What Bro I been ready," said 40.

"I got FO for that," said Cash.

"Then whats up?" he asked.

"Well later on I'ma have some smack that I need moved, can you handle that?"

"Do a bear Shit in the woods and wipe his ass wit a white rabbit?" asked 40, "hell yeah, I got you just hit me up when its go time."

"Aright my Nigg I'm out!"

Cash hung up as FO pulled into the parking garage that's underground where they kept the work vehicles; 15 non-descriptive Fords and Chevy's all Limo-tinted and all Throw-aways. They picked an 87 Ford Mustang, 5.0, loaded up and went to Mello's place.After they left Mello's place, it was time to punch the clock. When they reached Glover Street, they pulled in front of the stash house, left the car running, kicked the door in, bodied 3 runners and made off with $50,000 in cash and 3 bricks of raw heroine. All in all tonight was a good night and it was only 10pm. So, after splitting up the take, and hitting 40 off with the raw, they dumped the Mustang and tried to figure out a plan for the rest of the night. FO asked Cash what his plans were for tonight.

Cash replied, "We need to go out, cuz we ain't partied in 'Forever.'"

"I know," said FO, "so whassup?"

"How bout BWX Lounge?" asked Cash.

"Sounds like a plan to me," said FO.

"Good! Drop me at my crib, I'ma get dressed and scoop you up in an hour. I'ma pull out the 760 tonight!" Cash said.

"Don't pick me up, meet me at Momma Jefferies, I'ma drive my Vette tonight."

"Aright then!"

FO dropped Cash at his house and left to get dressed. It was time to party and relax. It was on tonight so the town betta watch out!

CHAPTER 4

Beautiful Girls

11pm on the dot Cash pulled up in his cream colored BMW 760Ll sitting on 24 inch Ashanti's. The interior was peanut butter and it was immaculate. He stepped out in an off white linen suit with a navy blue silk shirt and pocket square. On his feet were off-white Louie Loafers. He wore a Bezeled out Titanium Breitling, and 2.5 carat pinky rings with matching studs to complete his outfit. FO stepped out of Mrs. Jeffries in an all-black seer sucker suit with a white silk shirt open at the collar. On his feet were $1500 Ostrich shoes and the belt to match. FO sported a titanium Vulgari Watch, 1.5 carat pinky ring, a 12 carat Wonder Woman Bracelet, and 1.3 carat stud in his ear. His navy blue Corvette Z-06 was clean and waiting. The Kush was lit, the pills got popped and BWX was the next stop. Once they reached BWX Lounge *(The club between Baltimore and Washington D.C.)* it was paced and jumping. Cash and FO parked and walked to the front of the line. They nodded to the bouncer and slipped him 2 Benjamin's, instantly making VIP status. The DJ was spinning Nikki Minaj's hit, "Shitted on Em," and the crowd was killing the dance floor. The pills in their system and the Kush in their lungs it was go time Cash told FO to go get a booth he was going to the bar and when he returned they would go hunting.

About ten minutes later Cash came back with 2 bottles of Ace of Spade and 2 Pink Nuvo's. Once he made his way to the table and sat down the DJ switched records and was playing the new Wiz Khalifa and Snoop

Dog joint. FO had been eye-balling, 2 of the baddest chicks he seen in a long time. He quickly put his man on point.

"Cash do you see what I see?" asked FO.

"Where?" asked Cash while sipping champagne.

"On the dance floor over by the mirrors!"

They both looked at the 2 dime pieces making eye contact and smiling. One was brown skin, 5'5" tall, and measured a good 36-28-40; she had the most incredible smile Cash had ever seen, not to mention the body. The other was, dark skin about 5'7", 38-34-38 with hazel eyes and she literally had FO drooling.

"I see them now," said Cash.

"So, let's do this shall we?" said FO as he and Cash and made their way toward the two ladies, while maintaining eye contact.

When, they reached their destination it was time to spit that game. Cash was the 1st to take action.

"Hello beautiful, I'm Cash, and you would be?"

"My name is Cherice but, you can call me Reecy," she said, "this is my friend Kelly, and your friends name is?"

"Oh... Right... This is my right hand, his name is FO," said Cash.

"And FO, is short for what?" asked Kelly.

"FO' Pound, you know like the pistol?"

"Oh so I guess y'all are gangstas then huh?"

"No not exactly, but don't you think it would be better if we went back to our table in VIP, have a drink, and get to know each other?" asked Cash.

"What you think Kelly?" asked Reecy.

"It can't hurt Reecy unless these gentlemen bite!"

"Only if biting is wanted, or needed and even then, we only nibble," stated FO with a smile.

"Okay then, let us Ladies go to the little girls room first, then we'll be ready to join, you," said Reecy.

"That's cool," said FO, "we'll be waiting."

As the ladies went into the bathroom, FO being ever so suspicious of everything, and everyone asked Cash, "What do you think Bro? Do you trust them?"

"Calm down Nigga, can we get a chance to feel them out first? You may just enjoy yourself and get you some goo, new pussy instead of Fucking your fingers tonight," said Cash and laughed.

"Fuck you Clown," said FO, "it ain't like we squares dawg."

"I know what you saying my Nig, but they don't know nothing about C-4 so stop worrying and have some fun, Aright?" said Cash.

"Aright Man," said FO.

Meanwhile, in the bathroom Reecy pulls out her iPhone and makes an urgent call.

"Yes, this is Agent Cherice Thomas reporting in to Central District, Deep Cover Agent #316472. I'm currently in Baltimore pursuing open leads to see where they take me. Any correspondence or attempts to contact me should be made only through Mobil Email. My GPS is on and my emergency panic beacon is on my person, I will report in as needed with any relevant information that I uncover. My civilian contact is Kelly James, CI #74218. End of Report, I will call again with details."

And with that Agent Cherice "Reecy" Thomas, hung up, erased the number and then she and Kelly fixed their makeup and left the Ladies' Room.

CHAPTER 5

1st Impressions

When Kelly and Reecy returned from the Ladies' Room they were surprised to see that Cash and FO had ordered a seafood platter and already had 2 bottles of Champagne and 2 pink Nuvo's on ice and waiting.

FO said, "Welcome to VIP ladies, this ain't Burger King but you might can have it your way, please have a seat."

They made small talk and managed to have a good time with Kelly without being too suspicious.

"So Mr. Cash what is it you do for a living?" asked Reecy.

"Well Mrs. Nosey Lady," he smiled, "I'm an independent contractor/ consultant, meaning that I help entrepreneurs solve problems with their businesses."

"Oh Really?" she added, "and what kind of problems would those be?"

"Logistics problems, infrastructure problems, whatever is necessary," said Cash.

"Now how about yourself, Miss Reecy? With your nosey ass, what do you do for a living?" asked Cash.

"Well, if you must know, I'm in school for Business but, I've been known to dabble in Cosmetology when I need a few dollars," responded Reecy with a smile, "in fact, my partner and I are the bomb when it comes to hair and fashion."

"I see that, y'all both think y'all the Shit but me and my dawg got it on smash too," said Cash with a smirk.

"Yeah I've been peeping you and your man's style, I think y'all are cute too."

"I think those two are feeling each other too," she said motioning toward FO and Kelly.

"Yeah I see them, I think they're a little bit tipsy too," said Cash. Just then the DJ announced, *"Last call for Alcohol!"*

"So Miss Thang what else you got planned for the night?"

"Not much Cash why? What's on your dirty little mind?" joked Reecy.

"Oh I was just wondering if you had a curfew or can you hang out a little longer, that's all?"

"Well Mr. Cash what makes you think I'll go home with a man I just met, and on the 1st night at that?" asked Reecy jokingly.

Even through Reecy was feeling Cash a lot, she still felt the need to play hard to get.

"Reecy, I just figured that since we both grown and unattached that I would try my hand," said Cash, "but, I can understand if you not feeling it. Then can I at least have your number?"

"Hold on Fast Ass!" said Reecy, "I never said yes or no; I just asked you a question, slow your roll before You miss out on a good Thang!"

"Oh well EXCUSE ME, My Bad!" said Cash, "but check out your drunk-ass home girl and my drunk-ass homeboy.

FO and Kelly were really tipsy and giggling like school kids when they both caught themselves and glared at Cash and Reecy.

"What the Fuck y'all two nosey Mothafuckas looking at?"

"We ain't bothering y'all! Damn take a picture it'll last longer," slurred

Kelly before her and FO dissolved into a fit of hysterical laughter.

FO looked at Reecy and Cash and said, "I don't know about y'all but me and my Chocolate Easter Bunny bout to bounce on you two Clowns, holla at you when we smile at you."

Then Kelly and FO got up and made their way to the parking lot.

"Well, I guess that settles it, you're stuck with me for the night," stated Cash.

"I've been worse off, Mr. Cash so I guess I'll be okay," joked Reecy.

CHAPTER 6

Pay Back

The sunlight was wreaking havoc on the hangovers that Reecy and Cash just happened to be nursing at 9 o'clock the next morning. Reecy tried to block out the onset of the coming day by borrowing deeper in the down comforters and hiding her face under the soft goose down pillows. Cash on the other hand was feeling a little bit frisky this morning. He pulled Reecy's caramel, toned, fair skinned body towards him and into a strong but loving embrace.

"Don't even try it Mr. Slickness you can't have any of my candy, the store is closed!" teased Reecy.

"I'm the cat burglar don't make me break in and steal all your goodies," laughed Cash.

Reecy turned over towards Cash and said, "At least you still look good the morning after, so I'm not disappointed."

Cash said, "I'm going to kiss you now and since we both have morning breath it may taste tart."

"All talk no action is what you are," she teased they began to kiss slowly.

Cash kissed her forehead first, then her eye lids, and then her nose. Once he made it to her lips Reecy couldn't contain herself anymore she thrust her tongue into Cash's mouth and they kissed deep and hard. Cash then took the time to relieve Reecy of his oversized white t-shirt that she had slept in; Reecy took the liberty of removing Cash's wife beater and boxers Cash resumed his kissing, making his way down Reecy's sweet warm lips to her neck, then down to her breast. He cupped her left breast in his hands playing with her beautiful erect brown nipples teasing them until Reecy let out a sensual moan and reared her head back in ecstasy. Cash took her right nipple into his mouth and began to softly suck and caress it with his tongue and warm mouth.

"Oh yes! Mr. Cat Burglar, are you going to steal my cat," cooed Reecy.

Cash only responded with, "Shhh."

He then trailed sweet kisses from Reecy's ample breast down to her navel. He stopped when he caught sight of Reecy's beautifully shaved love mound. He looked at Reecy with a smirk and stated, "Breakfast is served."

Cash used his two index fingers to spread her moist lips. He began to lick and suck on her clitoris. He used the two index fingers on his right hand to slide in and out of her pussy until her juices dripped down her inner thighs.

"Oh My God! Daddy, what are you trying to do to me? I'll be a good Girl I swear I will," moaned Reecy.

Cash only smirked again as she savored the taste of Reecy before she exploded into dizzying waves of tremors.

"Oh Shit! I'm Cumming!" screamed Reecy as she laid on her back.

Once the tremors had subsided Reecy rolled Cash onto his back and said, "You think you nice wit it huh? It's my turn now!"

Reecy began to trail her tongue from Cash's chest down to his washboard abs stopping to tease his navel. She grabbed a hold of manhood and began to stroke it slowly. Cash immediately began to stiffen even more under Reecy's stimulating touch. Reecy began to tease Cash around the head of his dick with her tongue. She traced from the head, along the shaft to the bottom. She gently massaged his nut sack as she made circles around his balls with her tongue. Just when Cash couldn't take to anymore Reecy took all of him into her mouth and deep throated him.

"Oooh Shit Mommi Damn it," moaned Cash.

Now it was Reecy's turn to respond wit, "Shhhhh."

Reecy continued her assault on Cash's manhood until Cash was about to buss. Reecy slowed to a stop took Cash out of her mouth and proceeded to climb on top of him and lower herself on his manhood until Cash was completely inside of her.

Cash then came to life. He grabbed Reecy around her waist and began to thrust himself deeper into her each time she slid up and down. Reecy began to buck tremor again Cumming fast and hard before collapsing on the bed. Cash took this time to change positions laying Reecy on her back with her legs in the air. He plunged himself into Reecy again slowly at first until she began to grind back. Then he changed up the temp going deeper and harder as well as fast and slower, until Reecy, once again began to buck and shake in organism.

"Daddy what you tryna do to me?"

Again Cash said, "Shhhh!"

He then turned Reecy over on her stomach and brought her up on her knees. He entered her once again this time doggy style. Reecy was bucking like a Bronco. Her head swinging wildly from side to side as she moaned and repeatedly said Cash's name. Cash went as deep and as fast as he could until they both exploded in one big intertwined organism, and they both lay spent and curled up in the fetal position.

Reecy turned towards Cash and looked deep into his eyes and said, "Boy I don't know what your motives with me are but, if you hurt me now I Will Kill You!"

Cash responded, "I don't know about you Mommi, but, I play for keeps and you my Dear are a keeper."

They lay cuddling and giggling before getting up to shower and make love again. Reecy was in Heaven, there was only one nagging problem on her mind she had been compromised and she was falling in love. Two things that were never supposed to happen to deep cover FBI agent. She had to come up with something, and fast. Then she smiled to herself, she was resourceful, *"This ain't nothing I can't handle."* She thought, *"I just have to take control of this situation because my Mr. Right will not be going to jail for nobody."*

CHAPTER 7

6 Months Later

"Cash wake up Baby," said Reecy with a smile, "time to eat Baby!"

Cash and Reecy had been living together for the last 6 months and so far, everything was beautiful. Business was a little slow so he and FO had just been on cruise control. Just as Reecy had become Wifey for Cash, FO and Kelly had become an item. Today, was Sunday and Reecy, Kelly, FO, and Cash were expected at Mama Jeffries house for Sunday Dinner. Mama Jefferies was so delighted that the boys had settled down, with two nice, respectful young ladies that she didn't know what to do. Every chance she got, she teased the boys about it.

"Come on Baby wake up and eat so we can get dressed, Mama Jeffries is waiting on us," said Reecy.

"Ok Ree, but promise me that after I finish breakfast, I get an early dessert," he said with a kiss.

"Boy what you trying get me knocked up or something?" laughed Reecy.

"What's so bad about that?" asked Cash with a smirk.

Just then, Cash's work phone rang. He got up, grabbed the phone and went in the bathroom to take the call.

"Yeah?" answered Cash.

"Your Target's name is Omar an up and coming crack dealer trying to flood West Baltimore blocks... His location and schedule will be texted to you once you provide the account info for the money transfer."

Cash hung up to text his account info and called FO to let him know that tonight C-4 had a job.

As Cash was taking his call in the bathroom, Reecy was listening from the other side of the door. Reecy knew she would have to give her boss at the FBI something to go on soon, but what? She needed to make a move and fast. She had to do whatever possible to protect her man, her job, and both of their lives. The more she thought about it the more she knew she had a plan. All that needed to be done was to find out where this job was going down. She thought, *"Tampering with evidence is a small price to pay for our happiness!"*

"Cash, Baby your food is getting cold!" she yelled.

"Here I come, Baby!"

Cash exited the bathroom and he began to eat his scrambled eggs, turkey bacon, and waffles. He ate his food with one hand and fondled Reecy with the other. After the mid-morning make out session that followed breakfast Cash headed for the shower. Reecy told him to start without her so that she could lay out the clothes that they were going to wear. Cash went into the bathroom and turned on the shower, took off his clothes, and stepped in. Reecy, after laying out the clothes, grabbed Cash's iPhone and found the info she needed. She then made a phone call to a friend who owed her a favor in Evidence Control.

"Tony, this is Reecy," she said, "what do you have in the way of smuggled evidence?"

"A few assault rifles from an unsolved case why?"

"Those will be perfect, bag them up for me," she said.

"What are you up too?" Tony asked.

"Oh nothing, I'm just going to close that case for you, so if you have any more evidence from that case give it to me!"

"Thanks Babe, now I owe you one."

"Do what you do, I don't wanna know about it," he joked before hanging up.

Later she would report in to Lt. Gaines and throw him a bullshit bone to make it seem like she was hard at work. Then she joined Cash in the shower and made love to her man before they got dressed and left the house.

CHAPTER 8

Run Interference

"Dinner was the bomb! Mama Jeffries," said Cash.

"Yeah Ma, you musta put your pinky toe in that one," laughed FO while rubbing his swollen stomach, "Kelly, if you start cooking like that I got a big ass engagement ring with your name on it."

"In that case, child I got some family recipes for you too," laughed Mama Jeffries.

"Now how about you two young ladies help me get the kitchen and these dishes together?"

"Yes Ma'am," both girls answered.

Cash and FO took the opportunity to call Mello and make sure their order would be ready to go by 10pm.

After dessert, they cleaned the kitchen and prepared to leave; Cash told FO that he would meet him at the office after he dropped Reecy at the crib.

FO said, "Aright, I gotta drop Kelly off too, so I'll be there in 15 minutes."

Reecy asked, "Daddy do you, have to go to work tonight!?"

"Yeah Boo, but only for a couple of hours, then I'll be home to snuggle up with my Baby," he said to Reecy.

FO turned to Kelly and said, "Yeah Babe it'll only be for a little while, then I'll be home and you can have all of this!"

"What you mean to say is, you can have all of This!" said Kelly wiggling her ass.

Cash laughed and said, "I know y'all love us, and can't get enough of this Grade A Shit but, we do have to work unlike some people we know."

"Whatever Niggas," said both girls, "y'all just better hurry up!"

After dropping the girls off and going to pick up the guns and ammo from Mello, Cash and FO met at the spot and prepared their plan. The location was a house on Reisterstown Rd. and Ruskin Ave. The Mark was a crack dealer named Omar. Omar had pissed off quite a few hustlers on the block when he moved in and started selling half a grams for $20. C-4 wasn't concerned with that. Their only job was to remove Omar. Cash and FO were staked out in a vacant house 3 doors up on the opposite side of the street. The plan was simple once Omar arrived at the stash house and went inside, Cash would hit the front door and empty his Assault Rifle into anyone that didn't cooperate. FO would do the same as he entered from the rear of the house. What C-4 didn't know was that tonight they had a guardian angel in the form of Agent Cherice Thomas.

"Heads up FO," said Cash.

"I'm on it my Nigga," said FO after watching Omar enter the residence.

FO slipped out the back and made his way down the alley to the back door of the stash house. Cash simply put on his mask cocked his AR-15 Assault Rifle, walked out the front door of the vacant, crossed the street and kicked in the front door of the stash house catching Omar, his 2 thugs, and the crack head home owner off guard. 20 seconds later the back door crashed in and, FO appeared masked up AR ready!

"Everybody put y'all face in the Fucking carpet," said Cash.

"Make any funny moves and stop breathing," said FO.

"What the Fuck is going on!?" screamed Omar.

"Oh Yeah, if it isn't the man of the hour, Mr. Omar. Get up off the floor Big Man but, keep your hands up," said Cash.

"What's this all about?" asked Omar.

"I talk... You listen!" said Cash, "where is the Money and the Shit?"

"What Money? What Shit? I don't know what you mean?" said Omar

"Oh Ok, FO, show Omar what we mean," said Cash.

FO raised his AR and shot the first thug square in his face, blowing bits of skull and brain matter all over the carpet, next he shot the second thug in the back of his head smearing what was left of his face into the carpet too. The lady crack head was hysterically crying and peeing in her pants by this time. FO silenced her with a 3 round burst that damn near decapitated her.

Cash then asked Omar again, "Where is the Money and the Shit?"

Omar fearing for his life responded, "The 2 duffel bags are in the basement, one is money and the other contains 10 bricks. Please don't kill me!" he whined.

"Don't worry Omar, I won't kill you," said Cash, "FO, keep an eye on this Bitch while I go get these bags."

Omar began to sob and piss his pants.

"I've cooperated wit y'all man please, can I go now?" FO never said a thing; he just waited for Cash to return.

Cash came up from the basement after about 5 minutes with 2 duffel bags and a black book bag. "Looks like Omar was trying to keep some extra cash for himself," said Cash.

"Ok, Ok, Ok it's yours too. I'm sorry... Can I go now? You, said you wouldn't kill me," begged Omar.

"Oh I'm not going to kill you Omar," said Cash.

"Thank you, Thank you, Thank you," said Omar.

"Hold on Omar I said I wouldn't kill you, my partner is another story," said Cash.

FO shot Omar blowing the confused look on his face all over the walls and floor. They picked up the bags and left through the rear of the stash house. They jogged to the car, loaded the trunk, unmasked and quietly left the scene. At the same time Reecy (Agent Thomas) was on the phone with her boss, Lt. Gaines, explaining how she had uncovered a series of gang hits on drug dealers. She gave the location address and before hanging up she told him she would be in contact when she uncovered more info. Then she popped the trunk and removed two assault rifles she had picked up from Tony. Both weapons had blue flags tied around the barrel and stock. There were so many partial prints on them that they were sure to throw any investigating agent for a loop. Reecy sprinted up the block to plant the weapons in the house before the cops could arrive. She witnessed a gruesome murder scene while placing the rifles but, she didn't have time to take inventory. Reecy left like a bat outta hell because she had to beat Cash home and be gone before the cops got there. Phase one of her plan to keep her man safe was in the works. Phase two was next. *"Who knows maybe it'll work,"* she thought as she drove home!

CHAPTER 9

Surprise! Surprise!

C-4 had pulled several more jobs over the past 3 weeks. Five total, and each time the scenario was the same. FO and Cash did the job and without their knowledge, Reecy planted more evidence.

Cash and FO never knew the difference they thought that they had caught a lucky break when the cops and the Feds announced a joint task force to investigate gang members for the jobs that C-4 had been pulling off. Now though it was time to lay low for a few weeks and let the heat die down.

Cash and FO had cooked up a good surprise for the girls and now all they had to do was spring it. The plan was to take the ladies to the Bahamas' on vacation but, Cash had an even bigger surprise in store for Reecy.

"Baby how have your on-line classes been coming along?" asked Cash.

"Hectic as a bitch Baby but, I can handle them why? Whassup?"

"I just see you all stressed out and I think you need a break," smiled Cash.

"Oh Yeah, what kind of break? We already screw like jack rabbits!"

"No, not that kind of break Baby, even though that's a good idea," laughed Cash.

"Here," he said handing her a plain white envelope. Reecy smiled and opened the envelope to reveal two round trip tickets to the Bahamas.

"Oh My God! Baby, are you Serious? I really do need this type of Break… See, that's why I love you Boy!" screamed Reecy.

"I love you too Ma. Here," he said handing her, the keys to the 760 and 10 Grand in cash, "go pick up Kelly and y'all go shopping for the trip, and you buy all my clothes too, Ok Baby?"

"Yes Baby I gotchu," said Reecy reaching for her phone to call Kelly.

As the phone rang she kissed Cash for what seemed like the hundredth time.

"Hello!?" said Reecy.

"Bitch is you ready to go to the Bahamas?" asked Kelly, "I'm on my way to get you, so we can tear the mall down; be ready in 15 minutes."

Reecy hung up, got dressed, kissed Cash again and left to go get Kelly, with Reecy gone Cash could go and pick up the other 2 gifts he had without her being nosey. Cash slipped on a pair of black 7 jeans, a white and black Polo shirt, and a pair of white and black Prada shoes. He went to the safe in the closet and took out $120,000 and closed the safe. He placed the money in his Louie bag, and headed for the garage. He decided that he would take his 99 Mercedes SL-500 so that he could trade the Coupe in as partial payment for Reecy's second gift. He hopped in the car started it and pulled out of the garage. He drove out to Owing Mills, MD and pulled into the Range Rover Dealership.

"Nice Car," said the salesman as Cash was getting out the Benz.

"Thanks, I'ma miss her though," said Cash.

"Oh Really, you thinking of getting rid of it?"

"Yeah I guess so, I'm going to settle down so I wanna get Wifey her own vehicle."

"What did you have in mind?" asked the salesman smelling a sale.

"How much for that Champagne Range Rover Sport over there?" asked Cash.

"Are you sure you don't want to see something cheaper? I mean I'm prepared to offer you Fifty Thousand for your Mercedes but, that truck is Hundred Grand," said the salesman.

"Please White Man, don't disrespect me! If I asked about that truck then that's what I want," said Cash with a trace of anger in his voice.

"I got $60 Grand cash, take the car, you keep 10 for your tip and gimme my keys!"

"Oh, yes Sir, I'm sorry Sir, I didn't mean to offend you Sir. Right this way I have some papers for you to sign at my desk.

After getting the truck detailed and leaving the dealership Cash went to pick up surprise number 3. Cash pulled up to a jewelry store called Charles Nusinov, North East Baltimore. He went inside and straight to the counter.

"May I help you Sir?" asked a rather attractive Italian chick, with a smile.

"Yeah I'm here to pick out an engagement ring for my Lady," said Cash.

"Well, do you have something in mind or would you like me to show you something?"

"How much for that one right there?"

"I see you have excellent taste Sir, this 3 carat round cut Diamond and

Sapphire ring is set in a platinum band and retails for around $60,000," said the sales woman.

"Good I'll take it. I have 60 Grand cash right here," replied Cash.

After purchasing the ring and insurance Cash pulled out his phone to check on Reecy.

"Hello!?" said Cash.

"Hey Daddy, Whas Good? You Miss me?" asked Reecey.

"Always Baby, I was just checking on y'all," said Cash.

"We're still at the mall but, I got almost everything, I got you some cute stuff too, what you doing?" she asked.

"Nothing special, make sure you call before you leave because I got another surprise that I don't' want you to spoil, Okay," said Cash.

"Aww Daddy, Okay I will. I love you Baby," she replied.

"I Love you too," said Cash.

After hanging up, Cash drove to the house backed to truck in the garage, put a big red bow on the roof, then, went into the house. He laid out his black Hugo Boss suit, black and white Stacey Adams, and a black Fedora. For Reecy he laid out an all-black Vera Wang Strapless dress and a pair of black Jimmy Choo Strap up Platform sandals, that he bought Reecy the day before.

He then went into the bathroom and sat candles all around the tub. He laid out a Victoria Secret Bra, a Boy short set, and the Tommy Girl perfume. Then he spread Rose Petals from the front door to the bathroom and left cards in each room wit specific instructions, he smiled to himself and walked into the kitchen.

Act I

Once in the kitchen, he took out 2 Fresh Porter House Steaks, two Pounds of Jumbo Shrimp, and some Alfredo Noodles. He wasn't the best cook but, he wasn't the worst either. He began to season the steaks, steam the shrimp, boil the noodles, and chop fresh vegetables. He smiled to himself thinking, *"I must be in love cuz this girl got me cooking and Shit."* Two hours later as he was finishing up his phone rang and he answered,

"Hello."

"Daddy I'm on my way, I'll be there in 15 minutes," said Reecy.

"Ok Baby Girl listen close, when you pull up leave all the stuff in the car, park in front of the garage, go to the front door and follow the directions taped to the door."

"Directions, what are you up to?" asked Reecy.

"My plan, your surprise! You'll find out soon enough."

"Ok Baby, I can't wait, I'm on my way bye Baby."

"Bye," said Cash.

He raced to the bathroom and lit the scented candles and ran the hot bubble bath for Reecy. Then he set the table and got dressed. Reecy came in and did as she was instructed, she blushed and loved every minute of this mysterious pampering. She enjoyed her bubble bath, put on her new Victoria Secrets, sprayed on her new perfume, and dressed in her killer new outfit and shoes. As she read the last instruction card she happily made her way to the kitchen to see what awaited!

CHAPTER 10

Welcome to My World

Cash had set the table for two with each plate laced with homemade Shrimp Alfredo and a well done butter flied Porter House Steak. The wine was chilled, the glasses were frosted and the only thing missing was Reecy. When she stepped into the dining room Cash greeted her with a hug and a warm kiss. He offered her his arm as he escorted her to her seat before seating himself. Once they were seated he grabbed the remote the remote from his inner pocket and hit play on the iPod stereo. Luther began to sing that *"A chair is still a chair even when no one is sittin' there. But a chair is not a house. And a house is not a home..."* And he smiled at the lovely sight of his lady as they began their intimate candle lit dinner. After the Steak and Alfredo Cash got up, cleared the plates and refilled the wine glasses. He made small talk with Reecy to divert her attention as he slipped the ring from his pocket into her wine glass and proposed a toast,

"Baby, you know how I feel about you right?"

"Ok well tonight I just wanted to show you how much I appreciate you and Love You."

"Awww Baby... I Love You too."

"Then let us drink to US."

"Yes Baby to US then."

They clinked their glasses together and drank till the glasses were empty. As Reecy was finishing the last of her wine she noticed two things, Cash was down on one knee, and there was something in the bottom of her wine glass. Immediately Reecy realized what was happening and began to tear up. She looked in the bottom of her wine glass and gasped at what she saw. Cash as if on cue began the second part of his speech.

"Reecy before I met you, life was dull and boring but, you brought the sunshine back into my life. The only question I have left now is… Will you be mine Forever? Reecy will you Marry Me?"

"You Mothafuckin Right I will!" said Reecy.

And then the waterworks began. Cash stood and placed the ring on Reecy's left ring finger and kissed her again.

"Now that you have surprise number two, I have one more thing before we eat dessert," said Cash.

"But Daddy I don't need nothing else I have you and that's all I need," said Reecy.

"Nah not quite Baby, no wife of mine is going to be riding around in that Old Chevy beater you got, so here take this," Cash said while handing Reecy a car key.

"Oh My GOD! Cash you didn't have to do this!"

"Yes I did, now go look in the garage."

Reecy jumped up kissed Cash and ran to the garage only to be stunned at what she saw. A 2011, Champagne, Range Rover Sport. Cash appeared behind her in the garage with a smirk on his face.

Reecy looked like a kid at Christmas. She was so happy, she couldn't stop crying.

"Daddy I don't know what to say."

"Baby you already said yes."

Reecy's mind was racing she'd never expected to get engaged, this had all started as part of a case. Now she had fallen in love and was engaged to be married. What more could a woman want? She made up her mind, she was not going to lose Cash to anything or anyone, in her mind happiness transcended all. Even if it meant quitting her job and going on the run. Cash was her soulmate and she would die for him.

CHAPTER 11

Back to Business – 2 Weeks Later

It was the last day of the best two weeks in Kelly and Reecy's lives. They both had been proposed too, they both had been pampered, and they both agreed that their job didn't mean Shit when compared with their happiness.

Reecy filled Kelly in on how she single-handedly steered the FBI's investigation away from ever centering on Cash and FO. She laid out the rest of her plan to keep the Fed's running around in circles until she could figure out how to close this case. Reecy continued to report in to LT. Gaines with bogus Intel about her non-existent and manufactured case; she just prayed it would continue to be enough until she could end it. Kelly let Reecy know that she would play her part also. They both then agreed to enjoy the rest of the vacation because come tomorrow it was an early flight back to Bmore.

The next morning the two happy couples returned to Thurgood Marshall BWI Airport and collected their luggage. They all hugged and said their goodbyes before going their separate ways.

Cash kept asking if his future wife enjoyed her vacation and was she well rested. Reecy said even if they didn't go to the Bahamas she would have enjoyed herself with Cash, maybe not have been so well rested but yes she enjoyed herself with him.

Cash smiled kissed her forehead and said, "Good cuz you gotta drive us home."

"Why me? Come on Daddy."

"Your Truck so you're STUCK!" he laughed.

"That's the only reason you bought the damn thing cuz you was tired of driving Punk," said Reecy.

Cash loaded the luggage looked at Reecy smiled and said, "Home James."

After the short drive from the Airport, Reecy and Cash arrived at their home. Reecy hit the button for the garage door and pulled her truck in alongside Cash's BMW. Then they exited the Range Rover and Cash began to unload the luggage. Reecy made a beeline for the door trying to escape the task of helping Cash unload the truck.

"You think you Slick don't you? Mrs. Johnson will still have to pull her own around here you know," said Cash teasingly.

"I know Daddy but, I just have to pee really bad," whined Reecy.

"What's up wit you and your bladder lately? You sure have been peeing a lot!"

"Shut up Nigga before I pee on you."

"Promises, Promises, I might be down for a golden shower wit your kinky ass," joked Cash.

"Ewww, you nasty Fucker If I pee on you, you don't think I'ma still hit that do you?" laughed Reecy.

"Girl you'll still gimme some if I had on pissy clothes and shitty boots, now get over here and kiss me."

After unpacking and putting away their clothes and souvenirs, Cash and Reecy ordered take out, called FO and Kelly and then settled in to catch a movie on cable and to relax.

"Did you enjoy your surprises Baby?" asked Cash.

"Yes Daddy. I feel like the luckiest girl in the world," said Reecy.

"You betta have enjoyed yourself cuz you expensive as Shit."

"Boy what I got between my knees makes up for a couple dollars," said Reecy seductively.

Cash reached over and put his arm around Reecy pulling her close. He cupped her chin and tilted her face up towards him.

"Baby no denomination of bills is worth what you mean to me, you taught me that even a gangsta like me deserves happiness and for that I am grateful."

Cash pulled Reecy's lips to his and their tongues began to dance the slow grind of the Tango.

Cash's hands found their way under Reecy's shirt to the clip at the back of her bra. He fumbled until he released it freeing her voluptuous but firm C-cups, then in one swift motion they were both topless. Reecy was giddy as a school girl; she was still amazed at how Cash made her feel like a teenager all over again. Cash kissed Reecy more passionately as Reecy's hands found their way past his zipper and into his boxers and began to massage his manhood. Cash, now moving with more of a purpose, began to caress and assault. Reecy's erect brown nipples with his lips and tongue. Each circle Cash made around her nipple with his tongue sent waves of heat shooting into Reecy's dripping love box. At the same time Reecy had stroked Cash's manhood to life and right now he was harder than Chinese arithmetic. Cash knew what Reecy liked so he obliged. He licked his way down to her swollen clit. He teased all around it before he began to suck and nibble on it lightly. Instantly Reecy came in violent shuttering spasms, "OH MY GOD Cash right there! Baby Right There!"

That outburst gave Cash the needed boost to up his frontal assault on the pussy. Cash began using two fingers in the pussy along with his tongue. Reecy began to grind and buck her hips against Cash's face and fingers and before either of them knew what happened Reecy was shuddering again, "OOOOh Baby I'm Cumming again. Oh Shit, Shit, Shit Yeah," moaned Reecy.

After the last tremor had subsided Reecy said, "You lay back Sir, now your Ass belongs to me."

Reecy gently pushed Cash back on the couch and began to finish undressing him. Once she finished she took the time to admire the scenery. The slight of Cash's muscular body turned her on even more. Not to mention the sight of his 9 inch swollen Mandingo Spear.

Reecy didn't hesitate she couldn't wait to taste Cash so she took him all the way into her warm wet mouth, defeating her gag reflex, and began to work her tongue and throat muscles. Cash's eyes rolled back into his head and he was speechless. Reecy's head was so good that Cash was temporarily retarded meaning; coherent speech was out of the question. Reecy continued to work the shaft top to bottom, while using her tongue to tease at the same time. After about 10 more minutes of this treatment Cash began to quiver, he tried to speak only to get a sound like "DWAAHH" out of his mouth before exploding in Reecy's mouth and throat. Cash was sweating and spent, he tried to rest but Reecy was not finished yet.

"Mr. Right, I ain't through playing Bad girl!"

Reecy grabbed his softening member and began to tease and blow on the tip until she had coerced it back to life. Cash couldn't believe how hard she had him that fast, Reecy then slid herself down onto his shaft as Cash's breath caught in his throat. Reecy gasped, then moaned, she loved the way Cash filled all of the space inside of her; to her it felt like a hand in a glove. Reecy rode Cash so seductively and so good that they climaxed together and lay spent on the couch. Shortly after, they both drifted off to sleep.

CHAPTER 12

Phase II

Neither awoke until the next morning, still naked and cuddling on the couch with the TV watching them.

Good morning Baby, you was in rare form last night huh?" joked Cash.

"You can't Fuck me all the time, sometimes I gotta Fuck you Daddy," teased Reecy.

"Now that's something any man would love to hear, I hope to hear that more in the future," said Cash.

"Anytime, Anyplace I don't care who' around."

"OK I hear you Janet."

"Mrs. Jackson if you Nasty," teased Reecy as she made her way to the shower.

"Baby put the clothes in laundry room and after I shower I'll make breakfast."

"Yes Dear," said Cash being smart.

"Good at least you already know your place!" yelled Reecy playfully from the bathroom.

Just then Cash's work phone rang. Reecy listened from the bathroom as Cash took down info for the next job and then as he relayed the time and location to FO. After she showered and dressed she waited until Cash got in the shower, and then snuck in to the bedroom to verify the job info on his iPhone. An 8 o'clock hit on 2 dope boys down on Park Heights Ave and Belvedere Ave in Northwest Baltimore. Phase two of her plan involved letting the police, FBI task force get to the targets before C-4 could complete the hit and heat the now cold investigation back up. By the time Reecy stood in the kitchen making breakfast she had already relayed the info to her boss. LT. Gaines who was as we speak, gearing up to take down two suspects in an ongoing gang/murder for hire investigation. Little did he know that even though his suspects would have guns and drugs present? The hit scheme that they would say that they knew absolutely nothing about, would be the absolute truth.

Cash called Mello and placed an order for 4 Walther P-88 fully automatic pistols with extended 50 round clips and the usual stage 3 body armor, and black no-mex masks. He called FO and was on his way to pick him, the order, and the car up. Once he pulled up out front he called FO's phone.

"Hello," said Cash.

"Oh hey Cash, my Mr. Wonderful said he'll be right out."

"Whassup Kelly? Tell your pussy whipped ass man I said Hurry up," joked Cash.

"Shut up Nigga look who talking," laughed Kelly.

"Man, Fuck botha y'all, you and that long head mothafuckin' man of yours."

"Yeah whatever Clown, Boy he's coming out right now."

"Aright Baby Sis, take care."

"OK Cash Baby."

Cash hung up just as FO stepped out the front door. 45 minutes later

Act I

C-4 was locked, cocked, and loaded; the time was 7:45pm and they were watching the stash house from the second floor window of a vacant building across the street. A black Escalade had just circled the block twice slowly before pulling into a parking space.

"Two huge Gorilla looking Black dudes got out of the front and opened the back doors. Two more brown skin average size dudes exited the rear carrying book bags and one medium sized duffel bag most likely guns and money," said Cash.

"I say we storm in, kill everybody and leave, I ain't in the mood to search for work and all that Shit," said FO.

"That because your Pussy Whipped ass is getting lazy!"

"Cash, we got a nice piece of change stashed and hella drugs already, what else do we need?"

"Boy that Pussy got you lazy and half-crazy; I remember at one time you couldn't get enough doe, now Boy I tell you, you..."

"Nigga Fuck You! Don't act like this Shit ain't getting old. We got families now and I don't know about you but for the 1st time Shit feel Good!" said FO seriously.

"Aright Playboy don't bust a gut I feel you, I'm just saying keep your head in the game cuz I need you focused, a few more jobs and we can throw in the towel," said Cash.

"Now that sounds like a plan, that's what I needed to hear so let's get this one over with cuz my Baby keeping it warm for me, you'd still be jerkin off at night to Cherokee and Belladonna."

"Yeah OK, remember I spotted them in the club, Nigga."

"Yeah you right but I'm the one who... Oh Shit Look!" said Cash.

Just as Cash and FO were about to finalize their plans for the hit unmarked police cars, several cruisers, and a helicopter swooped in and arrested their marks and raided the stash house while they watched.

"What the Fuck just happened Cash?"

"The Fuck if I know FO."

Cash and FO were forced to stay put and watch as the FBI and the city Police booked their marks, collected evidence, and canvassed the scene. Cash cursed to himself under his breath as he thought about how close he and FO came to being on the wrong side of service weapons. FO leaned against the wall and began to contemplate his job, Kelly, and how close he came to going to jail. *"Something had to change and fast,"* he thought. This was too close.

After having to wait 3 hours in that vacant building, Cash and FO drove back to the spot, stashed the equipment in the trunk of the car and were about to go their separate ways...

"Cash what happened tonight?" asked FO.

"I ain't got a clue Brother," said Cash.

"Either that was a sign or somebody is on to us Cash."

"Come on FO don't go soft on me now we almost to the promise land Baby."

"Yeah I hear you but, I just got a bad feeling you know?"

"FO between you and me, we setting on almost 2 million dollars in cash and about that much in drugs, now I think we would be able to retire forever with a few more jobs, what you think?"

"Cash you have never steered me wrong since we were kids, you know I'ma ride with you, but let's take it slow man tonight was a little too close!"

"OK my Nigg, you got that," said Cash.

On the drive back home Cash got a call from his Lil Brother 40.

"What's good Lil Nigga?" said Cash.

"Not Shit, I was calling to let you know I got that paper for you and to see if you can get me a deal on a few bricks."

"Whoa! Time out you talking wreckless!" Cash hung up.

"What the Fuck is 40 thinking talking like that on my phone!" he said out loud. Let me slide thru there and check my Lil Bro cuz something ain't right.

Cash made his way over to Northeast Baltimore and pulled up on Harford Rd and Belair Ave. Once he parked he reached under the seat and picked up his Desert Eagle and cocked it. He put the canon in his pants, zipped up his leather jacket, stepped out and called 40's phone back,

"Hello!?"

"I'm out front, open up."

"Oh, OK Big Bro my bad."

40 buzzed Cash into the apartment building and Cash pulled the D.E. from his hip. He made his way 40's apartment door all the while listening for anything out of place. Satisfied that everything was cool he knocked on 40's door. When 40 opened the door and saw his brother with his gun out, 40 pulled his signature Smith and Wesson Glock 40 and rushed out the door.

Act I

"Hold up Lil Bro, I thought you was in trouble by the way you was talking on the phone, that's why I'm strapped."

"Oh I thought one of these Clowns in this building wanted some Rec or something," said 40 loud enough for his neighbors to hear.

"Come in Bro."

"So whassup with you?" said Cash after 40 had closed the door and handed him a black book bag containing 100 Thousand Dollars.

"Nothing Man I ain't mean to talk crazy on the phone, I'm just stressing a lil bit right now, you heard me?"

"Stressing bout what Lil Nigga?"

"Nah I need more work to feed my Lil Niggas cuz it's this dude name Money Bags, who tryna lock Shit down and we starting to feel it."

"Well what y'all need? And who the Fuck is a Money Bag?"

"1st answer is we need like 5 squares, 2nd answer is some new King Pin Nigga on the come up and he tryna squeeze out the Lil Niggas," said 40.

"Oh Ok, well you know that's 125 Nigga and you still owe me 50 already, don't make me hafta clap my Lil Bro," laughed Cash.

"Nigga I got you!"

"Aright I'm get them to you tomorrow and oh yeah Congratulate me Boy, I'm getting Married!" smiled Cash.

"You getting, what?"

"You heard me, I'm getting hitched Boy I got me a Winner."

"Damn, I know FO ain't feeling that."

"Shit FO bout to Jump the Broom too."

"Oh Hell Nah, what the Fuck I Miss?"

"I wish Mom and Dad was here to see this," said 40.

"Me too Shawty but, look I'ma let you meet Reecy tomorrow, I'ma have her bring you the work, just keep ya hands off my property Nigga," laughed Cash.

"I ain't promising you nothing, you know I'm the cute brother anyway."

"Boy your ugly Lil Ass... I outta here I Love you dawg."

"Love you too."

Cash called Reecy on his drive back across town she said she felt like takeout tonight instead of cooking. He asked how she felt about Fast Food and she said she wanted Checkers, she said she wanted a Kosher Dill Pickle and some Butter Pecan Ice Cream for dessert. Cash teased her about her dessert but he stopped and picked up everything before heading home. Cash had time to think on the drive home and he was desperately trying to come up with an exit plan from this dangerous game that he and FO' played for a living. He figured with a few more jobs and his savings, he and Reecy could relocate to Atlanta, buy a house, and open whatever business they could think of. The thought of Reecy never failed to make him smile and he was determined to be the main reason that she smiled. She had already become the center of his world he just hoped she felt the same. Cash finally pulled up to the house and parked. He was met at the front door by Reecy in her house robe and fuzzy pink Bunny Slippers.

He kissed her and made the remark, "At least my wife looks good without makeup, in a robe and slippers."

Reecy smiled and took a bow and said, "Thank you kind Sir."

Act I

Once they finished dinner and dessert Cash brought up the subject of moving to Atlanta. Reecy was psyched about the idea more than Cash would ever know. The thought of Cash leaving the game meant, she no longer had to lie, cover for him or for that matter she could quit the FBI. The more they talked the more it became a solid and stable plan. They talked about areas to live in, types of businesses to open, etc. They were even toying with a time frame in which they would move. Reecy really began to smile to herself and say, *"Thank the Lord!"*

CHAPTER 13

Meet the Fam

During the next week Cash stayed home and researched Atlanta. FO and Kelly had been over numerous times to compare notes of the plan just as they were doing today. Cash and FO were looking up homes and business opportunities on-line to see what was available in Atlanta. Cash spotted 2 that peeked his interest. The 1st was a barbershop/hair salon in Downtown Atlanta and the other was a 3 bedroom 2 1/2 bath single family home in Clayton County complete with a 3 car garage, basketball court, and a pool. After showing both to Reecy, he made a call to the Realtor and paid the closing cost on both without telling anyone else.

C-4 was about to take the ladies out for lunch and an afternoon movie date.

"Y'all ready to GO?" asked Cash, "because Reecy you driving."

"Cash I don't wanna drive, I feel like Shit I gotta throw..." Reecy dashed off to the bathroom.

"Kelly go make sure she's okay Baby," said FO.

"Yes ah please!" begged Cash.

Kelly followed Reecy to the bathroom and tapped on the door hearing Reecy wretch her brains into the toilet.

She tapped again, "Open up Girl it's me," she said.

Reecy opened the door then turned on the water and wet a face rag.

"Bitch how far along are you, and does he know?" asked Kelly.

"I don't know and no, he doesn't so shut your Fucking trap!" snapped

Act I

Reecy.

"When you gonna tell him?"

"When I find out for sure."

"You know the answer already," said Kelly.

"I just wanna be sure first."

"Ok cool, now about work, what we gonna do?"

"Kells I'm working on it, just bear with me okay."

"You know I got your back Bitch, I just wanna be pregnant too."

"Shut up Bitch! Let's Go."

After making sure Reecy was okay the four of them left and headed downtown to Fells Point. Reecy wanted pizza so they had lunch at the Famous Brick Oven Pizzeria in Fells Point. When lunch was over they made their way to the movie theater at Arundel Mills Mall in Severn, MD. The girls made their gangstas watch a chick flick and neither man complained, they would do whatever as long it meant spending time with Reecy and Kelly. When the movie was over they all decided to take a stroll through the mall and do a little shopping before heading home. Cash and Reecy went to the Nike Outlet and ended up buying 2 pairs of Nike boots and 2 pairs of Foam Posites. FO and Kelly on the other hand made their way from shop to shop until FO had more bags than Santa Claus.

On the way back to Baltimore, Cash received a call from 40 asking what time he was going to meet his mysterious new sister-in-law. Cash told 40 he would call him once he got home and see if Reecy was up to the task today. Cash hung up and then glanced at his Baby Girl sitting in the passenger seat.

"How you feeling Doll Face?" he asked.

Reecy smiled, shrugged her shoulders and said, "Perfect as long as I'm with you Handsome." Then she leaned over and kissed his cheek.

From the back seat came, "Please stop it or else, I'm gonna be sick," joked FO.

"Kells please kiss this pet gorilla of yours so he can stop being jealous," said Cash and then they all laughed.

As soon as they arrived back in the City they dropped Kelly and FO at their car and promised to get up with them later.

Cash then looked over at Reecy and said, "Baby I need you to do two things for me."

"And what two things are those?"

"Well 1st my Little Brother want to meet you finally."

"And!?"

"Well since you going to meet him, I want you to drop off something and bring some money home."

"Oh, so now I'm your errand Girl huh?"

"No it's not like that, I just figured we could kill 2 birds with one stone."

"We huh? You ain't slick, what am I dropping off, drugs, guns, what?"

"What you will be doing is handling Family Business while meeting your Lil Brother for the 1st time."

"Yeah OK whatever, don't make this a habit!"

"Yeah, OK my ass! Stay on point and watch out for my Lil Brother he think he a Ladies man."

Act I

Cash pulled up to the house got out and put a black duffel bag in the trunk, he kissed Reecy and told her to hurry and pick 40 and his homeboy up from the Metro Stop and drop them off on Harford Road. He called 40 and told him Reecy was on the way, he gave him a brief description, told him to keep his hands to himself and not to make her wait. They laughed, and joked until 40 had Reecy in his sight, then he hung up and got himself ready to go and check on the money in his safety deposit box and the money in his bank accounts.

Reecy pulled up to the Rodgers Ave Metro Stop and saw 2 young men waiting out front. It was a medium brown skin handsome man that stood about 5'5 or 5'6 with gangsta style cornrows in his hair, the other was dark brown 5'7" with an athletic build wearing a Khufi and a mean mug.

They waved then approached the passenger side as Reecy unlocked them.

"Ooh wee you must be Reecy, no wonder my brother has been hiding you from me, you look good enough to eat!" said 40.

"Hello 40 and yes, I'm Reecy how are you? And who is this with you?"

"Oh, I'm sorry Beautiful, this right here is my right hand, his name is St. Louis. He don't talk much but, he ain't to be played wit either."

"Well hello St. Louis."

"Sup?"

"O-K, 40 how was your day so far?"

"'Good' but it's gotten 38 times better in the last few minutes," he said smiling.

"Boy Stop! Flattery will get you nowhere!"

"Aright but do you have a sister?"

"No!"

"Lonely mother, desperate aunt or a feisty grandma?"

"Boy you retarded, you know that?"

"I call that, the family charm," 40 smiled.

"Sis can we stop at the next gas station? I gotta get my cigarillos."

"Only if you pump my gas for me?"

"You got that Big Sis, pull into BP and hold your money I got you."

"Thanks Lil Bro."

"You pay, I'll pump," said St. Louis.

40 handed Reecy the book bag and got out of the truck. She put it on the floor and watched as 40 spit his game to 2 other females and scored each time. She watched and wondered if the unborn fetus inside her would turn out to be a lady killer like his crazy uncle or would it be a pretty little girl like herself. She was snapped out of her daydream when St. Louis got in followed by 40 who slammed his door.

"Boy watch my doors this ain't no hoop-tie you know," stated Reecy.

"My bad I was just thinking that's all."

"Yeah I know about them 2 broads you just booked, I seen you."

"Guilty as charged," he smiled, "sis put my number in your phone and don't hesitate to call me for anything, you heard me?"

"I got you Lil Bro."

"I mean it; I got my Lil wrecking crew too, besides me and St. Louis there's 4 more of us. You got that?" said Reecy.

After 10 more minutes Reecy had dropped 40, St. Louis, and the duffel bag off and was headed home to Cash. She picked up the phone and dialed her boss for an update.

"Yeah!" he said.

"It's me," Reecy answered.

"Anything new?"

"Not so far, What about on your end?"

"No confessions they claiming innocent but, we got Federal fun and drug charges so that's a plus, but I want the leader Thomas!"

"I'm working on it Boss."

"Keep me posted."

"I will Boss."

Reecy hung up and called Cash and said she was on her way home and did he need anything? He said all he needed was her and that she should hurry home so that she could put her $50,000 away.

"My what?" she asked.

"The money in that bag is yours and I don't want you riding around with it so hurry home," said Cash.

"Oh Baby you spoil me too much, I'll be there in 10 minutes, be naked and aroused okay?"

"Say no more Angel. Hurry up."

They both hung up. Reecy couldn't stop smiling, she had never been treated this good. "NOT EVER!"

CHAPTER 14

Another Close Call

Another slow week had passed before Cash's work phone rang again. It was 6pm Monday evening. The hit was sanctioned for an El Salvadorian named Pablo, operating in South Baltimore. He was a dope connect and his stash house was located on Ramsey Street and Payson Street. Effective immediately the contract expired at 1am the next morning. Reecy laid beside Cash playing possum. She had heard the details of the hit and committed them to memory. Cash got up to get dressed went into the bathroom and called FO.

"Nigga it's go time, you ready?"

"Be ready in 10, I'll be outside," said FO.

"Aright Bet, make it 15."

Cash got up and gently shook Reecy.

"Baby I gotta make a run I'll be right back okay?"

"Okay Baby, bring me back some French Vanilla Ice Cream okay?" said Reecy.

"Okay Baby."

Cash then went to take a quick shower. Reecy used that few minutes to text Lt. Gaines and tell him where to locate another suspect or possible victim in this investigation and she explained that it was urgent that their agents moved fast. She then turned off her phone and turned on the TV. Just as Cash walked out of the bathroom, he dressed, kissed her and left. Reecy silently prayed, *"Lord Save my Baby and make sure that hit never takes place. AMEN!"*

Cash picked up FO and drove to the spot to pick up the vehicle and the tools from the last botched job. This time they wouldn't hesitate. They made up the plan on the drive across town it was simple, pull up in front, kick in the door, kill everything inside except kids of course, collect the money and drugs then escape untouched and unseen into the night.

"Have you figured out how many more jobs we need before we quit?" asked FO.

"Could be 2, could be 1 big one, I guess we'll have to see what the take is when it's over," said Cash.

"Oh OK I figured as much, anyway, me and Kelly found a nice house in ATL, but, I need that Realtor's name that you used so I can grab the house tomorrow." "Cool, I got you on that, don't even worry bout that," said Cash.

"Cash did you ever think a time would come when we would want to retire from the game?" asked 40.

"I knew one day I would but, now that I got Reecy I'm ready to straighten up and fly right!"

"Yeah we still Cruddy Buddies til the end but I'm ready to be a daddy," said FO.

"What? Did I hear your gorilla faced ass say you ready to mate?" joked Cash.

"Yeah you heard me, Mama J said she ready for grandkids so I'ma give in."

"I feel that Shit, you tighten up though it's almost show time, let's get focused cuz this is the BLO…"

"What the Fuck? Police! Cash keep driving." "I see em' dawg."

Just as Cash and FO were about to turn into the block and go to work they noticed the whole area was blocked off and the helicopter was circling again. Cash quickly banged a left and put some distance between them and Ramsey Street, before they ended up at an address that they would regret later on.

"Cash that's the second time man What the Fuck is going on?"

"I don't know but I'm starting to see things your way more and more FO, that was another close call."

"So what we gonna do?"

"We gonna pick and choose from now on, 1 last big job and then we outta here." "That's what I wanted to hear," said FO.

C-4 decided to keep the tools but dump the car since it had been used twice. Once they changed clothes and were back in the 760, they both made calls home to check in. They discussed bits and pieces of the exit plan before Cash dropped FO off and went to 7-11 for Reecy's ice cream.

Reecy breathed a sigh of relief that Cash and FO were okay and not in jail. She was worried that Lt. Gaines hadn't acted fast enough and that C-4 would be caught in the act. Now the only thing left to do was to figure out on, who when and where she would plant her remaining evidence and then bring this case to a close before quitting so she could open up a new chapter in her and Cash's life. Atlanta, marriage and a family all sounded like heave to Reecy. *"Soon,"* she said to herself, *"soon it will all be over."*

CHAPTER 15

A King Pin

Meanwhile across town, Money Bags aka Jerrod Sims, sits in his home office feeding stacks of 20's, 50's, and 100's in the money counters on the table. His main 2 bodyguards, Scooter a 6ft 5in 380lb monster, and Greasy a 6ft 5in 320lb monster kept watch over their Boss. Money's second in command is also present. His name is Earl.

"Boss so far everything is moving according to schedule, majority of the street crews over here gotta cop from us, we got the best product and the best price," said Earl.

"What you mean by majority of the street crews? Earl I want everybody copping from us," said Money.

"What's the hold up?"

"Well, there's only 3 hold out teams, The Belair and Erdman Boys, they are about to run out of product. The Old York Boys, we beefing with them, and the Harford and Belair Boys, they still got product and from what I hear its comparable to ours," said Earl.

"The Belair and Erdman Boys will join soon enough them Old York Boys; kidnap a few of them and take them to the warehouse and end that beef. Now these Harford and Belair Boys we gotta find out where they copping from and put an end to that. I want all North East money to touch my hands you hear me?" asked Money.

"Yeah Boss! Oh yeah the money from the 2 newest spots was picked up this morning, I think we should go up top and pick up about 50 more bricks just so we will have them when these Niggas is ready to re-up!"

"Make it happen Earl, pretty soon you'll have to run East Baltimore, because I'ma set my sights on West Baltimore so get ready," said Money.

"Boss since you got the new security system installed do you think it was wise to cut down on guards in the house?" asked Greasy.

"This Shit right here Greasy is high tech, not only is it an alarm system with camera's but this joint got face recognition software where it can identify anybody that got a record. Then you and Scooter can go and earn y'all's pay but, ain't nobody even tryna beef wit us, we taken over like DJ Khalid, you heard me?"

40, St. Louis, Samir, Raheem, Abdul Haqq, and Black Drew all sat around the table in 40's apartment smoking and counting up today's take.

"Fuck that Nigga Money, man we gonna stay self-sufficient as long as my brother is around," said 40.

"All I know is I'm straight with what we got and I ain't trusting that dude," said St. Louis.

"I heard he got a spot in an old warehouse downtown where he disappears Niggas," said Raheem.

"Man Fuck that clown ass Nigga. If we gotta bang out then we bang outwit em," said Black Drew.

"Well we still got 2½ of them things and work in the street once we get this 125 I'm gonna grab again and this time I'm see about getting some dope too," said 40.

"Make sure you holla at Mello so we can get our gun games back up too," said Samir.

Act I

"What y'all want me to do?" asked Abdul Haqq.

They all said simultaneously, "Shut up and roll the Got damn weed!"

On the other side of town Cash and Reecy were busy making plans to pack all their things up and get them ready to move to the house they had purchased in Atlanta. Cash had given FO the number to his Realtor and he and Kelly were about to purchase a home in Decatur. Reecy was so busy packing that she almost hadn't had time to finish formulating the rest of her plan. Lt. Gaines was still waiting on new leads to develop and he was pressing Reecy to find out whatever she could so that she could feed him more info. The more she tried to balance her double life, the more it became complicated, coupled with the fact that she was pregnant and her hormones were acting up. Life was getting hectic.

CHAPTER 16

The Beginning of the End

Cash and Reecy had been packing up the house for about 3 days now and everything was going according to plan; Kelly and FO were in the process of packing up their things too. Mama Jeffries was a little sad that they were moving but, when FO' offered to move his mother in with them until she found her own place she declined.

"Reecy we still have to figure out what to do with that old beat up car of yours," said Cash.

"Baby don't worry before we leave I'm going to give it away to charity but, I've got to clean it out first!"

"Oh OK Babe, you feel like running to the store for boxes, bags and possibly lunch?" asked Cash.

"Yeah Babe I can, what you want to eat?"

"You decide Reecy, but get boxes and stuff from U-Haul okay?"

"OK Babe I'll be back in a few."

As soon as Reecy pulled out of the driveway Cash's work phone rang.

"Yeah," he said.

"Your target is an E-pill distributor named Marcus. The location is on North Ave and Smallwood Ave in West Baltimore. Please provide us with the account information so that we will be able to wire your fee and conclude this transaction."

Cash provided the necessary info, hung up, and called his partner.

"Hello," said FO.

"It's on and popping Baby, we got one."

"Do you think this is the big one?"

"It could be, either way its money in the bank so get ready."

"Aright give me 15," said FO before hanging up.

Cash got dressed, left a message on Reecy's voicemail when he didn't get an answer, and then left to pick up FO. Reecy didn't get the voicemail message until 10 minutes later, and by then Cash and FO where long gone. *"Fuck!"* she said to herself, *"I hope that they make out OK because I don't know where they went."* She thought, *"One ain't gonna hurt the case but I gotta hurry up and close this case."*

Meanwhile, Cash and FO were halfway across town, they already had the equipment they needed, they only had to go to the spot and pick up a vehicle then they would head straight to North Ave and go to work.

"Cash, do you think we gonna be able to pull this one off?" asked FO.

"Man we should be aright, don't think like that, that Police Shit was only on a humbug Nigga, this what we do, so let's get it done!"

"You right my Nig, let's get this Shit done and over. What's the plan?"

"Same as always except this time we ain't gonna let them get inside the stash house, since the Police and Feds investigating gang hits and Shit, we make this look like a drive by."

"That sounds like a plan, so we gonna post up on the block till we see them pull up then what?"

"We pull up spray whoever there take what we want and peel, No Questions Asked."

"Aright let's do it then."

Act I

Cash pulled the Chevy Caprice up and parked on the corner of North Ave and Smallwood Ave across from a bar. Behind tinted windows Cash used binoculars to watch the area in front of the stash house, while FO kept a look out for Police, nosey people, or any other signs of trouble. After about an hour of watching, Cash said, "It's Showtime."

A Burgundy Dodge Caravan pulled into the block from the opposite direction, it was attempting to park as Cash eased the Caprice out of the parking space. They pulled their black no-mex masks down over their faces and cocked the automatic pistols. It was time go and C-4 was ready!

As the minivan was backing into the parking space, FO noticed there were 3 people inside 2 in the front seat 1 in the rear.

"I got the front seat Cash you get the Mark," said FO.

"Gotcha my Nigga," said Cash.

The 3 people in the van never looked at the Chevy Caprice twice and before they realized it the car was stopped beside them blocking them in and two figures masked up and dressed black hopped out and all hell was breaking loose.

As soon as Cash stopped the car FO was out of the passenger side door. He immediately raised the pistol in his right hand a sprayed the driver side door and window. There were at least 20 bullet holes in the door and window. The 1st 5 slugs tore the drivers face completely off splattering it all over the passenger. The rest of the shots had peppered the already lifeless body of the driver. The passenger panicked and tried to return fire only to get hit with 20 rounds from the 2nd automatic pistol in FO's left hand. The slugs damn near decapitated the passenger and left him with a bloody stump above his neck. Cash, by this time, had the sliding door open to the van was confronting a shocked and scared Marcus.

"Hand me everything you got, the work the money and whatever else you got worth value," said Cash.

"Here! Take all this Shit!" said a terrified Marcus.

Cash tossed the 2 big duffel bags into the back seat of the Chevy, and then turned around before Marcus could beg for his life he aimed both of his machine pistols at Marcus' face and squeezed both triggers at the same time. The last thing that Marcus saw was 100 hollow tip slugs disintegrating his face, neck, and chest. Cash and FO hurriedly jumped back into the Chevy amid the screams on the block, and hauled ass from the scene.

Approximately an hour later, Cash and FO had dumped the vehicle and the guns, changed clothes, and were in the process of splitting up the take.

"200 Grand a piece and 10 Thousand pills, that's a start," said Cash.

"Yeah I thought that was gonna be the one, but maybe next time," said FO.

"Nigga have faith, it's gonna come."

"I know dog I'm just ready that's all! They finished splitting up the take and left for home. Cash called Reecy and said he was on his way, the he hung up.

The next day Cash went to pick up his money from 40 and drop him and his team off another 5 Keys

"What up Lil Bro?"

"Not Shit dawg, what's good wit you?"

"Same Shit different toilet, Oh yeah I forgot to tell you I plan on moving to the ATL next month, so as far as me being your supplier I've decided to wholesale you the rest of the work I got. It should hold you and your team for a nice lil minute."

"Oh Shit that's whassup that mean we won't have to Fuck with this clown Nigga Money Bags."

"Again wit the Money Bags character, what so special bout this cat?"

"Man dude really tryna lock Shit down, Listen, he was beefing with the Old York Boys and his goons made them disappear."

"What you mean disappear?"

"Yo got this warehouse downtown I think they used it to make the lye plumbers use there, but anyway once they take you in you don't come out and they never find a body."

"So what is he leaning on y'all?"

"Nah, word is he tryna wait for our connection to dry up so we hafta cop from him but you just killed that plan."

"Well look you still got Mello on speed dial right?"

"Hell yeah!"

"Then I suggest you strap up cuz this cat sound like trouble."

"Oh best believe we ready for whatever."

"Aright my Nigga, keep me on point and I'll get wit you about the wholesale price and the pick update; oh yeah its 10,000 E-pills in that bag try not to eat em' all, I need all my doe Punk."

"I love you too, you Chump."

"I'm outta here Son!"

"I'll call you later, oh yeah kiss my sister for me, or you want me to kiss her myself?" joked 40.

"Yeah aright Nigga, I'm gone before I hafta hurt ya lil ass," said Cash as he hopped in the whip and went back home.

CHAPTER 17

Money Bags or Money in the Bag?

With everything in the house packed up and ready to move to Atlanta, Cash had his mind on looking to do one Last job and taking that money and running. He had wholesaled all his remaining drugs to his little brother, transferred all his accounts over to the same bank, sold off C-4's stash of vehicles and put his house on the market. Reecy on the other hand had yet to come up with a way to close her case, she had yet to come up with a way to tell Cash that she was pregnant, or to announce to Lt. Gaines that she was quitting. FO and Kelly were in one process of packing up themselves also.

At noon Cash and Reecy decided to take a break and Cash sent Reecy out to KFC to pick up lunch for them both.

"Baby get an original recipe bucket, mashed potatoes, rice and gravy, dessert, and 2 large sodas. Make sure you stop and grab me a pack of cigarillo's too," said Cash.

"OK Baby anything else?"

"Nah, at least not till you get back," grinned Cash.

"Now Yo talking my type of Shit," said Reecy with a smile.

Then she got her keys and her jacket and left. As if on cue Cash's work phone rang.

"Yeah," said Cash.

"Your target is an up and coming King Pin by the name of Money Bags, the location of the job is a house in the Randallstown section of

Baltimore County. This job is a little more difficult. The Mark has armed guards, alarm system, video surveillance, and armored vehicles. Due to this fact our original fee will be paid double. The time allotted for this job is one week due to the fact that you must stake out the residence, time the guards, and get to know his schedule. Please send your account info so that we may transfer your fee."

Cash hung up and texted the necessary info, next he called FO to let him know the ship had come in.

"Hello?" said FO.

"My Nigga you ready?"

"Ready for what?"

"The one we've been waiting for."

"Hell yeah I'm ready!"

"What you got for us?"

"I ain't gonna talk too much on the phone but, its a doozy."

"You want me to be ready?"

"Yeah but, not like you think, this one we gotta slow roll it."

"Oh aiight it must be big then I'm down, keep me posted."

"Nigga I'm on my way, we'll talk in the car."

"Aright, I'm OUT!"

Cash hung up the phone and smiled to himself, *"Only one more week and then I get to start my life all over, and with a new wife at that."* He got dressed, grabbed his keys, and a set of binoculars and left to pick up FO. He called Reecy and let her know something had come up and that he would be back before dinner.

Reecy took the phone call from Cash and was immediately disappointed. She thought, *"Damn that's the second job that I haven't been able to get rid of the rest of this evidence I have and Lt. Gaines already thinks I'm slipping. I've got to get this Shit done and over with so I can get on with my life."* Reecy called Kelly to see what info she had on this newest job.

"Hello," said Kelly.

"Whassup Bitch, what you doing?"

"Oh hey, Heifer I'm chilling why what's Good?"

"Did Cash come and get FO yet?"

"Yeah they just left. What you know about this newest job?"

"Not much all I heard them say was something about Money Bags!"

"Money what?"

"Bags Bitch, I guess they mean they're about to get paid, I don't know."

"I don't know what that could mean but I'm check it out."

"Aright Bitch let me know Whassup?"

"OK, Whore, I'm gone."

"Later."

Reecy hung up and called Lt. Gaines. He asked her was the hit on North Ave connected to their case, she told him yes and she was getting closer to finding out who the mastermind was. He told her not to blow her cover and to give him the info as soon as she got it. She acknowledged and hung up. She went home and promised herself she would concentrate on Phase III of her plan because she was ready for a new life.

Cruddy Buddies

Act I

Cash and FO had been staking out the Randallstown house for 2 days now and they realized that this Money Bags dude had a crazy ass schedule, 5 bodyguards and a 2nd in charge. Money was moved into the residence in an all-white work van. Work was moved from the garage of the gated property. C-4 was only interested in the Mark and the money. So they began to go plan out an all-out assault on this property. The beginning of the end is what they called it.

"Yo you see them camera's they got? 2 on the front gate, 2 on the house, and 2 on the back of the house," said FO.

"Yeah, but we can get onto the property through the woods in the back," said Cash.

"OK what about them guards and that Earl Nigga?"

"There are 2 guards at the front gate, 2 that walk rounds, and 1 at the rear of the house."

"I know!"

"The ones on the gate and the back doors don't move, so we gotta snuff the 2 patrols, then the one at the back door," said Cash.

"Then what?" asked FO.

"Then we enter through the back find Money Bags and Earl; do the last 2 guards on the way out."

"Sounds almost too easy, I never want to be on your bad side my Nigga, you're a tough Mothafucka," laughed FO.

"So I guess we watch and make sure the schedule don't change in the next 2 days, and then we move on Thursday," said Cash.

"And we can move out by the weekend huh?"

"Exactly!"

Cash and FO continued to watch the Money Bag's residence for the next 48 hours and began to make the necessary moves to pull off one of the biggest, If not the biggest hit in C-4 history.

Cash made up an extensive list of equipment he would need from Mello, then he called his Lil Brother to see what the word on the streets about Money Bags was without alerting him to the situation. He learned that there was no change to Money's everyday routine. He also found out that Money had at least 10 spots in the city pulling in at least 30 Grand or better a day. He thought to himself, *"That's at $300,000 a day!"* He hung up with 40 and called Mello to check on his order.

"Yo, Mello what's good?"

"Shit my Nigga, I'm ready for you, the sniper rifle and flash bangs just got here, everything else I had."

"Aright I'm see you in an hour."

"Done Deal."

They hung up and Cash called FO

"Whas good Fam?"

"Shit getting ready."

"OH aright that's Whassup, bout an hour and we get Money Bags from Money bags, you heard me?"

"That's what it is my Nig?"

They hung up, and Cash noticed Reecy staring all in his face.

"What's wrong Baby?" he asked.

"What's all this Money Bags talk, what you and FO talking in codes now?" she smiled.

"Nah Boo, that the name of some clown ass wanna be King Pin Nigga, ain't nothing big though."

OH OK, so what we doing today?"

"You gonna finish up around here and call the movers, this furniture gotta get moved Today."

"Why today, Baby?"

"Because tomorrow you gotta go and get rid of your old car and tie up other lose ends."

"OK but, why the rush?"

"Because we'll be in ATL by Monday."

"Oh My God! Baby are you Serious?"

"As a heart attack!"

"I can't believe this I got so much to do!" said Reecy and she literally meant that.

Reecy called Kelly and asked her could she follow her to drop off her old car to the charity for the blind tomorrow, she said her car was in the shop but she as pretty sure she could get FO to follow them and then to drop her back home. She told Reecy that she would keep her ears open for more info but right now all she knew is that FO had told her that Money Bags was their meal ticket, whatever that meant. Reecy put 2 and 2 together but it didn't do any good to alert Lt. Gaines because she didn't know a location or the situation and she could not and would not risk losing Cash and FO to an FBI sting. So she decided that she would have to make her move before the aftermath. All of the needed evidence was still neatly packed in the duffel bag in the trunk of her old car. Tomorrow she would back track and plant it at the scene somewhere. Then she would quit and move on with her life.

Cash left the house after kissing Reecy and picked up his partner. They went to Mello's place and picked up a 50 caliber sniper rifle, 2 flash bang grenades, 2 AK-47s, stage 3 body armor suits no-mex mask and gloves, and a suppressor for the sniper rifle.

"What we owe you Mello?" asked Cash.

"Just gimme 10, what the Fuck y'all doing anyway, going ta war?"

"Nah, we delivering somebody to Hell," laughed FO.

"I don't doubt that, by the looks of this order, I wouldn't wanna be him."

"Me neither," at that they all laughed.

"Look man we gotta get moving I'm holla at you later, you heard me?"

"That's cool y'all keep it tight."

Cash and FO loaded up and headed for Randallstown. They were in a black Ford Econoline 150 work van with tinted windows as they drove to the destination the plan was that FO would drop Cash and the equipment at the start of the wooded area behind the house, drive the van over to the block in front of the property and park it by the gate on the street. Then he would walk back to where Cash was waiting in the woods. Before they began the assault they would wait until they saw the drop off van arrive with the bags of money. Then they would wait an addition 15-20 minutes for everybody to resume their normal activities before they joined the party.

"FO the roaming patrols come every 10 minutes, they meet up on the right side of the house before they both turn around head back the other way, that's where I'm hit them with the sniper rifle," said Cash.

"Aright what about slim at the back door?"

"He's next to get it thru the door, He won't even matter."

"Okay, then what?" asked FO.

"We mask up go in through the back and search for Earl and Money Bags; Flash bang the house do our job, get the money and leave."

"So after we do them two Clowns what about the guards?" asked FO.

"We hit them and then you run and get the van and we out!"

At 9am exactly the cash van rolled up to the electric fence. Scooter who was in the booth, buzzed Greasy and the van on to the property. Greasy and one other guard from the guard shack at the gate began to take the bags inside the house. Earl met them at the front door and escorted them to the money room. Unknown to Cash and FO, Money Bags wasn't home he left late last night to go to Kentucky to visit his brother in the Federal Prison there this morning.

At 10:15am the normal activity resumed at the residence the guards began their rounds, Earl and Greasy began to count today's take and Scooter and the other guard watched. But in the front guard shack, Cash began to watch the roaming patrols through the scope on the rifle. FO made sure he was locked, cocked, and ready to go when the fireworks started. 2 minutes passed before Cash squeezed the trigger on the big sniper rifle. All you heard was psst, psst. At the same time, the two roaming patrol guards met on the side other of the house, each man looked in horror as a grapefruit sized hole appeared in the middle of each of their chests. By the time they both hit the ground the guard inside the back door's head exploded all over the wall behind him. Instantly Cash and FO burst from the woods and ran to the back door.

Earl and Greasy were so busy counting money that they didn't notice the commotion or the 2 black clad figures that approached the back door of the house and gained entry to the place. Scooter and the other guard had the TV turned up loud because they were jamming to the New Big Sean Video & Nikki Minaj. Cash and FO crept inside of the back door guns at the ready. They walked up the hallway through the back of the kitchen into the main hallway, listening for any noises that would tell them where the 2 men were. They began to hear the noises given off by the money counting machines and they heard muted laughter coming from the 2nd room on the right in the middle of the hallway. FO and cash crept on either side of the partially open door. On Cash's signal FO tossed a Flash bang in the room. The muted concussion blast and flash had the desired effect on the unsuspecting men.

As Greasy was in the process of passing Earl another stack of 20 dollar bills he noticed a black tubular shaped canister roll into the room and before he could ask Earl what it was, it exploded blinding them both and knocking the air out of their lungs. Before either man could recover enough to grab a weapon it was all over.

Cash kicked the door the rest of the way open and leveled his AK-47 at the fat man standing by the stacks of money, he reasoned this to be Money Bags and he opened fire hitting him in the back causing his lungs to collapse instantly drowning him in his own blood.

FO aimed his AK at the dude sitting in the chair rubbing his eyes and screaming FO sneered at him before blowing brain matter and skull bits all over the TV monitors behind him. Earl instantly urinated and defecated in his pants making the room stink horribly.

Cash went on to the next step of the plan. He went to the window to take aim at the guard shack. The guards didn't know it, but they were watching the last video they would ever see.

Scooter and the other guard were too busy watching the video for Lil Wayne featuring Drake "She Will." They never heard the flash bang or the AK47 fire coming from the house. The guard stood up, looked at Scooter and said.

"Man where these lazy ass patrol Niggas at? They should have made their rounds."

"They probably smoking a cigarette you know how it go, when the Boss is away the mice will play."

"I'm look and see where they at bef..."

In mid-sentence the guard's brains exited his head and colored Scooters shirt. He dropped to the floor minus half his head. Scooter pulled his Smith and Wesson internal hammer 357 from the holster but never got to stand up. The window exploded in front of him and he looked on in horror as he noticed the softball sized hole appear in the middle of his chest. Then he slumped over as his life drained away.

FO took off running toward the front door. He removed his mask thinking, *"I don't want the neighbors to see a masked man in black run out of here and get into a black van."* Little did he know the camera at the front door of the house caught his face and the computer began to run his mug shot thru its facial recognition software program. FO continued to the guard shack, stepping over the emaciated bodies and pushing the button to open the electric fence. FO slipped out of the guard shack and through the fence again, his face was captured in one camera. He started the black van and drove on to the property. By this time Cash had emptied the contents of the open safe, and began to stack duffel bag after duffel bag of money by the front door. He ran out of bags to place the money in so he used one of the queen sized bed sheets in the master bedroom.

FO backed the van across the grass to the front door and opened the back doors. He met Cash at the door, and began to load the bags with a smile on his face.

"FO where is your mask?"

"I took it off, so I wouldn't alert the neighbors."

"Well, I guess it won't matter since Money Bags is dead."

"Yeah and we rich; well I mean richer."

"Yeah, it looks like we hit the jackpot."

"How much you think it is?"

"It's probably 3 point 5 to 4 mil maybe more, that's why I grabbed the money machines too."

"Aright let's talk about this later we gotta dip before it get hot."

"You right, so move a lil faster wit ya lazy ass," joked Cash.

Once they loaded up they closed all the doors, got in the van and pulled into the street. FO stopped, ran back to the guard shack and closed the fence. Then they pulled off and drove back to the spot so that they could dump the van and the guns, count the money, and get ready to make their grand exit from the game, this life, and this City.

Act I

CHAPTER 18

When the Good Goes Bad

Money had finished visiting with his brother at about 11:30am. He was in the parking lot when he decided to call Earl and check on his daily operations. The phone rang repeatedly and went to Earl's voicemail.

"Earl what the Fuck is going on? You bet-ta not be slacking off or Fucking none of them hood rat ass Bitches of yours in my house Nigga, call me back."

He hung up and then he called Grease's phone, only to get his voicemail too. He didn't start to panic until he called Scooter's phone and got the voicemail.

"Driver, get me to the G-4 and A.S.A.P!" he told the guard he had driving him.

Cash and FO had dumped the van and guns and had just finished counting up 6 point 2 million dollars exactly. They smiled at each other knowing that this was just what the doctor ordered. They now had completed the last leg of their exit strategy. They would both be 4 mil and some change deep in retirement. All they could think of was the new life that they would live once they left Baltimore. FO's phone rang and he answered after seeing Kelly's number,

"Yeah Babe?"

"Where are you? You know we promised Reecy we would follow her to drop off her old car then bring her back to her house."

"I know Baby I'll be there in a few, so be ready."

"OK Baby, I love you."

"I love you too."

"Bye."

Cash looked at FO and laughed, "Duty calls huh?"

"Yeah I gotta follow your wife to drop off her car."

"What you gonna be doing while I'm doing that?"

"I'm going to take this money and get it into the bank so that we don't have this bulky Shit sitting around, what you want me to do with yours?"

"Put it with yours we'll sort it out when we get to ATL."

"Okay, let's put this Shit in the trunk of the 760 then I gotta call Reecy and the bank manager."

"Aright!"

They loaded the bags into the trunk and then Cash called Reecy and told her to be ready because FO was on his way to pick up Kelly and then meet up with her. He then called the bank manager and told him that he had an off the books deposit that he needed to make and asked how much it would cost him. Once they settled on a fee of 50 thousand, Cash left to meet him and FO went to get Kelly.

Money was on approach to Dulles in the G4. He still hadn't gotten in contact with anyone from the house and fearing the worst he called in a group of 5 back up soldiers to meet him on the tarmac as soon as he landed. He tried all 3 phones again before he called Hotdog the leader of his back up soldiers waiting on the ground.

"Yeah Boss, Whassup?"

"Are y'all at the airport yet?"

"Yeah we're waiting on you to land."

"Good, as soon as I do we go the house and check it out, I still haven't heard from Earl, Scooter, or Greasy so I guess it's safe to assume the worse. I'm hoping the security cameras caught something and if they did my facial recognition software should give us a clue to who we're after."

"Aright Boss I see your plane now, we ready and waiting."

"Aright, see you in a min."

When the plane had landed Money had the door open and was trying to exit before the plane had completely stopped. As soon as it did, he was down the stairs and in the back seat of the black armored Yukon Denali. Hotdog was in the passenger seat with one of his soldiers driving. The other 2 soldiers followed them in a black Jeep Cherokee. They exited the airport making a beeline for the expressway doing 90 miles an hour all the way to the Randallstown Exit off 695. When they turned on the street that the house was on, Money immediately noticed the drop van in the driveway and that the front door to the house was not wide open but it was cracked when they pulled up. Hotdog had one of his goons in the Jeep go up to the guard shack and open the gate.

After doing so he ran up to the passenger side window and reported the two bodies in the shack to Hotdog. When they got out of the vehicles, Hotdog had his goon's search the property and the grounds before he and Money stepped out. They reported that everyone was dead and that whatever had been in the room that Earl and Greasy were in was gone. Money instantly got upset, "What you mean gone, like there's nothing left!?" asked Money.

"There's nothing in the safe or in that room Boss, nothing but their bodies," said the goon.

"Take one other guard with you and y'all dispose of the bodies, driver, you clean up the blood and get rid of anything else you find," said Hotdog.

"Yes Sir," they both answered.

"Hotdog take me to the computer in my office so I can see who we gonna kill."

"You got that Boss come on."

Inside the master bedroom Money brought his Mac Book on-line and opened the face recognition software, immediately He was greeted with the mug shot of one Daniel Jeffries aka FO. It listed a Calvin Johnson as his known accomplice and it even had a current address for him. *"Thank God for the Internet,"* thought Money.

"Now all we gotta do is find this Cock Sucker and get my bread back," said Money.

"What kinda Niggas rob you but don't take the work too?" asked Hotdog.

"The dangerous kind," said Money.

"Let's Go! We got work to do!"

Money wrote down the address and everybody minus one guard, who was tasked with disposing of the bodies and the white work van, loaded up strapped up drove over to the address for FO.

FO had gotten to the house an hour earlier and showered. He was in the kitchen making a sandwich and waiting for Kelly to get dressed. The only thing on his mind was the job they had pulled 3 hours ago and thought of finally getting out of this city and away from this game. Kelly had finished showering and was dressing when her phone rang.

"Hello," she said.

"Whassup Bitch, you ready yet?" said Reecy.

"Yeah Slut I'm getting dressed now, FO is waiting on me, so come on."

"Aright I'm leaving now."

"Hurry up Floozy," laughed Kelly before hanging up.

While FO and Kelly were in the house waiting on Reecy. The Armored Yukon Denali pulled to the curb 3 houses up and sat idling.

"That's the house right there," said Hotdog.

"I see it," said Money.

"Now all we need is for this punk Motherfucker to come out of it."

"I got him leaving out to try and put the cash somewhere because nobody in the right mind would stash that in their house anyway."

"Boss we got Company," said Hotdog.

"Damn is that the Feds in that beat up Chevy?" asked Money.

"Nah I doubt it, it looks like it's just some chic."

"Heads up, they're leaving, let's follow them, we can make our move in a better area, with less nosey residents!" said Money.

Reecy followed FO and Kelly for about 20 minutes when they got to the Charity for the Blind. She pulled the car into the parking lot, got out, popped her trunk, and removed the duffel bag with her evidence in it. It contained 2 HK MP5's several hand guns, and about 10 blue Crip flags. She told FO to open his trunk and place the bag inside. Then she went inside to fill out the necessary paper work before returning to FO's vehicle, all the while no one noticed the black Yukon Denali parked across the street.

"What the Fuck we doing here?" asked Hotdog.

"I don't matter, once we leave here this punk Motherfucker and whosoever wit him is toast," said Money.

"That's Whassup we got the green light boys," said Hotdog to his goons."

At the same time Reecy had returned to the car and gotten in. They were headed back towards Cash and Reecy's house when Reecy asked FO could he make one stop before they dropped her off,

"Where?" he asked.

She said, "The CVS, I gotta grab something real quick."

"Aright I got you."

They pulled into the parking lot at the CVS on Liberty Rd and Rolling Rd in Baltimore County. As Reecy got out on the passenger side a black Yukon pulled along the driver's side. The passenger side windows and the rear door opened two men with UZ's and a 3rd with a Tech-9 opened fire on FO's car. Reecy ducked behind a parked Ford Taurus and drew her service weapon. As she watched in horror, the 3 men riddled the Lexus with bullets.

FO had just let Reecy out of the car and was looking for a specific track on the cover of his CD when he saw movement out the corner of his eye. Kelly screamed when she looked up and saw 2 men exit a black truck and another in the front seat point a gun out the window. FO reached for his 45 but never made it. Bullets ripped through the window hitting him in the side of his face blowing his brains all over Kelly's face, ending his days upon this earth. Kelly continued to scream hysterically until the man in the front seat armed his Tech-9 and squeezed 3 rounds into her open mouth blowing the back of her head on to the seat's headrest. Reecy had her Glock 40 in the ready position when she sighted the first man with tears in her eyes and hate in her heart she blew his brains all over the side of the truck. The 2 remaining men sprayed the Ford Taurus as they got ready to leave the scene. Reecy emptied her clip at the armored vehicle only to succeed in emptying it and being hit in the shoulder.

The remaining goon and Hotdog went into retreat mode once Reecy started to shoot back at them.

"Oh Shit that Bitch was strapped and she killed Pedro," said Hotdog.

"Let's Go! We got work to do before the cops show," said Money.

"You right Boss."

"Driver take me back to that Mothafuckas house Now!" said Money.

Reecy was still crouched down behind the car and bleeding when the thought hit her. *"FO and Kelly are dead and the evidence is in the trunk of the car. I hate to do this but, my best friend and her fiancé' are the scapegoats for this case to close, I know its Fucked up but they're dead so it won't matter to them,"* she though as she called Lt. Gaines for back-up and an ambulance. 10 minutes later Reecy was on a stretcher in the back of the ambulance where she had blacked out but not before telling Lt. Gaines that FO and Kelly were dead because FO was the mastermind behind the gang hits and that Kelly had been her contact in the case. That was why she was caught in between the crossfire when someone retaliated against FO for a hit. She managed to kill the gunman and that she had located corroborating evidence in the trunk of their vehicle.

Lt. Gaines congratulated her on the good work before she told him that this was her last case and that she was quitting because she was pregnant. He told her he understood and that he would take it from here. Then she passed out from the blood loss.

CHAPTER 19

From Bad to Worse and Back

Reecy was in ICU after receiving a blood transfusion. Her vital signs were stable. The baby was doing well but, she was still unconscious and dreaming of Cash...

Cash was at home after depositing the money. He was waiting on the movers and watching TV, he had called Reecy's cell phone only to get the voicemail and leave a message.

Money, Hotdog, and 2 goons had searched every square inch of FO's house only to come up empty. Money was getting very frustrated with looking for his money. He remembered that FO had a known accomplice name Calvin. He pulled out his Mac book used the WiFi and opened the face recognition software. He looked up the name of the accomplice and did an internet search and found the address he needed.

"Let's Move y'all! We got another date," said Money.

"Are we green lighting this Fool too?" asked Hotdog.

"Nah, this time we gonna take him to the warehouse, torture him, and when he tells me where my money is we drop him in to a heated vat of lye; his body will dissolve in 3 hours without a trace."

"That's whassup Boss, I like your style. Let's go."

2 hours later Reecy woke up groggy and looking for Cash. It took her a minute to realize where she was and when she sat up she caused several alarms to go off. The alarms sent the nurse running into her room. When the nurse entered the room Reecy asked 3 questions off the break."

Act I

"How is my baby? Where is my phone? And when can I leave?" asked Reecy.

The nurse nodded without answering as Reecy got out her bed amid protests.

Cash was watching a re-run of Real Housewives of Atlanta when his cell phone and the doorbell rang at the same time. He decided to answer the door because he was waiting on the movers.

Money, Hotdog, and the 2 goons were standing on the other side of the door when Cash opened it. As soon as he pulled the door Hotdog kicked it causing Cash to stumble and fall on his face. They rushed into the house and were on top of Cash before he could get up off the floor. One of the goons produced some zip ties and tied Cash's hands and feet. Money walked over to Cash after the goon had sat him up and hit him with the butt of his 357.

"You Lil Bitch you and your homeboy got something that belongs to me and I Want It!" said Money.

"I don't know what or who you're talking about," said Cash through clenched teeth.

"Yes you do, so did your homeboy Daniel before we killed him and his Lady friend."

"Killed who? You lying piece of Shit," said Cash.

"Oh yeah your Man, and his Girl are long dead, and whoever they Lil Home Girl is, I hope she bleed to death for killing my bodyguard," said Money.

"What? You shot the girl that was with em' too, Bitch I'm kill you when I..."

Money smacked Cash with the pistol again making his mouth bleed and said, "You won't do Shit cause by the time I get finish with you, you'll wish you were dead. Then you will be. Now, where the Fuck is my Money Bitch!?"

"I don't have any Money! Nigga Fuck you!"

"Y'all search this Mothafucker and if you don't find it, we taking this piece of Shit to the warehouse."

They searched the house and didn't find anything close to 6.2 million. So they put Cash into the back of the Yukon and left with him. Cash's phone still sat on the counter of the ram shacked house ringing, but never being answered.

Reecy began to get hysterical because Cash always answered his phone. Against the doctor's wishes she left the hospital and caught a cab home. After a 20 minute ride the cab pulled up to the front of the house, she paid the fare and got out. Once the cab pulled off, Reecy pulled her service weapon and made her way into the house, she noticed Cash's car still sitting in the driveway. She stepped into the hallway after pushing the unlocked door open. She called out Cash's name but got no answer. She quickly searched the rest of the house but didn't find Cash. Reecy noticed signs of a struggle and realized there was blood on the floor; she panicked before calming down and calling 40's phone, she didn't know what else to do.

The black Yukon pulled up to the loading dock of the abandoned lye warehouse. The 2 goons opened the back of the truck and half dragged and half carried Cash from the hatch to the building. Hotdog and Money followed the goons into the building where Cash was, they tied his arms above his head with chains and wrapped them around his hands. They hoisted him up so that he was suspended over a heated vat of lye. Then the torture began. Money produced a cattle pod and began to shock Cash savagely.

"Where the Fuck is my Money Bitch?"

Cash never answered he just took the abuse and readied himself to meet his Maker.

40 got his crew together and jumped in a minivan. They drove to meet Reecy at Cash's house. St. Louis drove because 40 was way to upset. Everybody else sat in the back seats and readied their weapons. Samir, Raheem, Abdul Haqq, and Black Drew were all armed with automatic assault rifles and Glock 357s. 40 had his Glock 40 and a Baby UZI, St. Louis had a P-89 and a Tech-9. Everybody was dressed in black and in a foul mood. 40 sat in the front seat remembering a sobbing Reecy on the other end of the phone saying something about Cash being missing, FO and Kelly being dead, and mentioning Money Bags. The last part was what had brought it all together for him is that it couldn't have been a coincidence that his brother was missing and Money Bags had been mentioned. He knew exactly where he would start this search and in his mind he knew he had to act fast because Money Bags made people disappear.

15 minutes passed before they had Reecy in the car and she was explaining what little she knew about the Money Bags situation.

"40 we were getting ready to leave this raggedy ass place, I was out running errands with FO and Kelly, when out of nowhere a truck pulled up; they killed FO and Kelly and shot me," said Reecy, pointing at her left arm in a sling.

"You sure it was Money and them?" asked 40.

"I'm positive 40!" said Reecy.

"How many we looking at with him Reecy?" asked St. Louis.

"I saw 4 others but I murked one of them."

"That's whassup Niggas, my Big Sis more gangsta then some Niggas I know Abdul Haqq," said 40.

"Man Fuck you Bama! We gonna see who gangsta and who not, just Hurry up and Get there!" said Abdul Haqq.

"Anyway, when the shooting start, Reecy I want you to stay put be..."

"Fuck that 40! Cash might be your brother but he's my life I gotta go in and get him."

"We got this Baby Girl, we don't want you to get hurt," said Black Drew.

"Say what y'all want, but I'm going in to get my Man!"

"Aright but Samir is going to go with you and watch your back."

"I got you Ma," said Samir.

"Aright let's get it my Niggas," said 40 about the Money Bags situation.

Money was getting tired of this game. Cash was going in and out of consciousness and he still hadn't given up any information. Hotdog sat laughing at all the pain that Money was inflicting on Cash. He had sent the two goons out on patrol around the building but he really wasn't expecting any trouble. Money jumped up and grabbed Hotdog's Tech.

"Bitch I'm through playing games, where the Fuck is my Money?"

Cash mumbled, "Up your grand ma's rusty asshole Bitch!"

Money got frustrated as shit and took aim at Cash's left leg and fired a 3 round burst.

Cash screamed as the lead hit his bone and splintered it. He began bleeding more than he was before. Just as the van with 40, Reecy, and his clan was parking, they heard the shots go off and began to exit with a purpose. Abdul Haqq jumped out of the van and without waiting for everyone else he ran up on to the loading dock and looked in the window. Everybody else decided to move together. They circled Reecy and began a slow but steady creep in the direction of the loading dock. Abdul Haqq turned around and said as loud as he could, "It looks empty to me!" Before he could say another word the window behind him shattered and his brain met with the pavement. Instantly everyone else took cover and tried to see where the shots came from.

"What the Fuck was that?" asked Money.

"I don't know Boss nobody know where we are, maybe them dumb Fucks is having target practice," said Hotdog.

"GO and check on these ass holes of yours before I take target practice on them!"

"OK Boss!"

As Hotdog approached the area where the shots went off he called out to his goons! What the Fuck is going on?"

"Some dude was snooping around so I shot him," said the goon.

"Anyone else?" said the other goon.

"Well now we gotta dispose of another body, so let's go get it."

Once the guards went back into the building 40 and his click split up and went on to the loading dock. 3 on the left side and 3 on the right side. When Hotdog and his 2 goons came out the doors the second time they were met by the barrels of 6 guns.

When Hotdog and the goons bent over to pick up Abdul Haqq's body all they heard was the cocking of automatic weapons. All they felt were barrels pressed against their backs and skulls.

"Where ya Boss at big Man?" asked 40 while pressing his Glock to one of the goons head.

"My Boss right here," said the goon.

"You know what the Fuck I mean Bitch where's Money at?"

"Inside of the warehouse," stammered the goon.

"SHUT up you chump ass Bitch, I got something for you...!" 40 smacked Hotdog with his Glock in the mid-sentence.

"You ain't gotta worry my Man, all 3 of y'all going the same place. St. Louis take their weapons, Raheem and Drew tie these whores up and stand them over by that wall. Firing squad style!" said 40 with a devilish grin.

"Samir and Reecy go see if you can find my brother and his host."

Samir and Reecy left the scene that was unfolding and went into the building. They crept up the hallway, Reecy with her 40 in hand, Samir with his AK47 cocked and ready. When they reached the doorway at the end of the hall, they peered through the window and what they saw made

Reecy's heart sink. Cash was hanging from the ceiling suspended over a boiling vat of lye and bleeding.

They watched as Fat Man savagely beat Cash and repeatedly asked questions but never got answers.

"You Lil Bitch you're gonna talk! You gonna tell me where my money is or I'm beat you to death!" said Money.

At that precise moment Money heard a bunch of automatic machine gun fire erupt from the area of the loading dock. It momentarily made him lose focus. And that fleeting moment would be his last mistake.

Reecy and Samir burst through the door at the same time that 40 and his click started shooting on the loading dock. Samir aimed at the Fat Man and sprayed his legs with the AK. He screamed and dropped to the floor on the opposite side of the vat. Reecy ran up to where they had the rope tied into the wall and tried to lower Cash.

Money laid on the floor whispering and begging for Samir not to kill him. 40, St. Louis, Black Drew, and Raheem came in to the vat room with the 3 dead bodies and tossed them in the vat of lye.

"They'll be dissolved in about 3 hours," said 40.

"40 help me get Cash down, Oh My God! Help me y'all," begged Reecy.

"St, Drew, Raheem help Reecy get my brother down, I still got a Pig to make bacon out of."

"Who the Fuck are you guys!?" screamed a wounded Money.

"I'll pay y'all whatever y'all want Just Don't Kill Me!"

"It's just like a Bitch Nigga like you to play tough at 1st then beg at the end!

"You know what? Fuck this piece of Shit pop off Samir!"

Samir raised his AK and 40 raised his Tech and they both emptied their clips into Money causing him to spasm and die.

Once they had gotten Cash down from the ceiling, he laid unconscious in Reecy's arms!

"Baby please Wake Up, I Love you. It's gonna be OK!" said Reecy.

"Cash can you hear me? I got something to tell you, I know you can hear me. You're got to wake up because I need you Boy!"

"Not only do I need you but this baby inside of me needs you too, so Wake Up!"

Cash tried to move and lift his head but he was too weak so he just opened his eyes and smiled,

"That's all you had to say Baby. I kinda figured you was pregnant but, I wanted you to say something First, well Mrs. Johnson did you enjoy the ride I took y'all on?"

"Shut up Boy you retarded! 40 we gotta get him to a hospital now!"

"Aright Let's Go! Y'all let's get him to the van," said 40.

"Oh yeah Reecy I'ma kick your ass too!" said 40.

"Why you say that Lil Bro?"

"You ain't tell me you was pregnant with my niece or nephew!"

"You still couldn't have stopped me from coming in here!"

"I know! Cuz once a woman get hooked on this Johnson family Dick they Go Crazy!"

At that they all left laughing at 40's retarded ass.

CHAPTER 20

Still Standing 6 Months Later in Clayton County, Georgia

"Baby, I'm miserable as shit, Help me!" said Reecy.

"I did help you remember? That's the reason there are two babies inside of you instead of one!" joked Cash.

"How could I forget?" remarked Reecy.

"I can help you make your water break if you'd like!" he teased.

"I bet you can, but you can't have any more of this pregnant pussy Boy!" she teased.

Just then the phone rang...

"Hello?" answered Cash.

"Whassup Big Bro? What's good down in the A?" asked 40.

"Not Shit Lil Bro, just working in my barbershop and waiting for the twins to come."

"How's Reecy?"

"She good, she's just miserable."

"I can dig it, everything is cool up here, we holding it down, I just wanted to touch base and stay in contact wit y'all that's all!"

"Tell all your Lil Homeys I appreciate everything y'all did and if you need me don't hesitate to call!"

"Aright Baby One!"

"One!" they hung up.

Cash and Reecy had moved to Atlanta as soon as Cash could travel. They had given Mama Jeffries all of the money that FO had stashed away in his safe deposit box. Then they packed up and disappeared. Reecy was no longer working with the FBI, and even though Cash had a lot of questions he decided that he had laid that life to rest and would concentrate on this new one. Life was good and looking better every day. He smiled, looked over at his newlywed bride and decided to take life slow and live it up to the fullest.

Meanwhile in a Kentucky Federal Prison, Money's brother Murder was just receiving his mail after count cleared. He had a letter that was postdated from his brother. When he opened it he read it and instantly got mad. The letter stated that if he was reading this letter now it was because his baby momma had mailed it out only because he was missing or presumed dead. Murder's mind began to calculate. He needed to make some phone calls and fast...

If his brother was dead or missing somebody was going to pay. Big Time!!!

ACT II

CRUDDY BUDDIES

CHAPTER 21

2 Years after Receiving the Letter from Milky...

Today was the day! Murder had been up exercising since 4am. It was now 8am and the CO. was standing at the grill waiting for Murder to grab his things.

"You ready Shit Bird?" asked the officer.

"Why wouldn't I be ready to get away from your ugly ass smiling?" asked Murder.

"Yeah, you Blacks never learn, you'll be back! That's why I have job security now!"

"Fuck you too! Cracker!"

"Open 32," said Smitty.

45 minutes later Murder had signed himself out and was exiting thru the prison gates with a check in one hand and a bus ticket in the other. In the back of his mind he thought, *"Now, somebody's gonna pay for what happened to my brother! I've been waiting for this day for the last 2 years!"* Then he began to flag a taxi.

During his 12 hour bus trip all Murder could think about is where would he start? Who would he ask, or what would he do? But, first he had to get in contact with Money's baby momma and see what she knew, yeah! That would be his starting point.

40 sat back and looked himself in the mirror as the hood rat bitch on her knees in front of him began to deep throat him like it was going out of style. He placed one hand on her back of her head and literally began to

face Fuck her. She let out a little moan and took it all like a champ, before 40 knew what had happened he came in her mouth and down her throat.

"OOOOOH Shit! Here it comes Tree, get it all Baby, get it all!" yelled 40.

"You like that Daddy?

"I'll do that for you anytime!" said Tree.

"I know Baby, that's why I love you," joked 40.

40 had taken over the Lower East Side of Baltimore City with the stash of bricks that his brother Cash had wholesaled him before he left. Now 40, his right hand man St. Louis, Samir, Raheem, and Black Drew were one of the most feared, lucrative, and respected drug organizations in East Baltimore. Even though they sold drugs for a living they gave back to the hood. St. Louis owned a couple of fast food carry out joints that employed High School aged kids, and a few of the neighborhoods recovering addicts. 40 owned 3 Laundromats and he too employed recovering addicts. Raheem, Samir, and Black Drew owned 2 auto detail shops and they too offered jobs to those in the hood. The Wild Boyz is what the hood affectionately called them but, don't get it twisted, as good as they were at heart, cross them and it would be 10 times worse! 40's phone rang.

"Yo!" he answered.

"Whas good my Nig?" said Mello.

"Mello, whas happening Baby?"

"Nada, I was just calling to let you know I just got a new shipment that I know you gonna want to see!"

"Oh yeah? What you got for me Baby?"

"10 brand new M-16 A2's with grenade launcher, grenades, and 5 automatic 12 gauge shotguns with incendiary rounds!"

"Incendiary rounds? Ain't they the one that catch on fire?"

"Yeah!"

"How much?"

"$35,000 for everything and the ammo!"

"You got a deal; St. Louis and Raheem will be to see you Shortly!"

"Why you gotta send St. Louis? That man scares the Shit Outta Me!" asked Mello.

"That's cuz St. Louis don't play any games and he don't have any cut cards but, I'll let Raheem pay you then and St. Louis can wait in the truck."

"Aright 40, if you say so."

"One!"

"One!"

Murder had just arrived at the Greyhound Station on Russell it's in Baltimore City. He went to the pay phone and called Money's baby momma, Milky. He told her where he was and she said she would be there to pick him up in 25 minutes. He hung up and went outside the bus station to buy a pack of cigarettes and to wait for Milky. Once Murder had walked to the gas station and back, he decided to go back into the bus station. Once inside he took a seat and put 50 cents into the TV on the chair where he was sitting and started to watch TMZ.

The smell of perfume made him look up and into the eyes of the most beautiful sight he had seen since he started his 5 year Federal bid on a gun charge. He saw a brown skin 5'6" cutey pie with measurements something like 34C-28-40.

"You must be Murder I can see the family resemblance, except you a little more in shape!" she flirted.

"And you must be Milky," he said.

Murder grabbed Milky's hand and kissed it. "The pleasure is all mine," he said and smiled.

Instantly Milky felt heat between her legs and even though she felt guilty to be truthful Money was dead and gone. Murder though he felt a vibe jumping off of Milky and, even though Money was his brother, he knew Money cared nothing for Milky when he was alive so he reasoned that he really wouldn't care now that he was dead. But that would have to wait till later because he had work to do.

"Do you have some place to go? If not you can stay in my spare room. Even though me and your brother weren't together he took care of me and your nephew. So you're welcome stay as long as you want! Shit, I need a man around the house anyway," said Milky, hoping Murder would catch her double meaning.

"I think I would like that Mrs. Milky, please lead the way," said Murder. She smiled as he took in the back side view that she intentionally presented to him.

CHAPTER 22

Getting Started

St. Louis and Raheem picked up the order from Mello's and were on their way back to the bat cave when St. Louis looked over and noticed the driver of the blue Honda Accord Coupe to his right.

"Oh Shit! Raheem tell me that ain't that Bitch ass Nigga Tony!"

"Damn, you right St. Louis; don't that Nigga owe us like 30 grand?"

"Yeah and that Coupe he's driving got temp tags on it. Take the Wheel!"

St. Louis jumped out the truck in the middle of traffic; Raheem slid under the wheel and hit the door locks because he knew what was next.

"Ay you Bitch ass Nigga! Where my Scrilla? You buying new cars but, you ain't paid me my Money? They can bury you in this then!"

St. Louis pointed his Glock 357 at the driver side window and caught the driver off guard and wild eyed. The 1st bullet shattered the glass and hit him square in the temple, the other 6 made mash potatoes out of his head and face. St. Louis jumped back in the passenger side and Raheem pulled off...

Meanwhile Milky and Murder were just pulling into the driveway of a 3 bedroom, 1½ bath Ranch style home in the Woodlawn section of Baltimore County. All during the ride Milky and Murder kept stealing little glances at each other.

"So Mister Murder, what do you plan on doing with yourself now that you're home?" asked Milky.

"Well 1ˢᵗ I'm get settled in, then of course I gotta find out what happened to my brother," he answered.

"I kinda figured as much, I'll tell you all I know and then if you need anything and I mean anything! Don't hesitate to ask me Okay?" she smiled seductively.

"Believe me Ma I won't hesitate but, let's go in so I can get situated and then we can talk."

"OK, you can have the room in the basement for now!"

"For Now?"

"Yeah, at least until I can't fight it no more and end up sharing my bed with you!" she seriously joked.

"Don't play wit fire Milky, It'll burn off your eyebrows Baby," said Murder.

"If you only knew Boy! Let's Go!"

They got out of the truck and Murder grabbed his things and followed Milky once again enjoying the view.

When they were inside and Murder had put his things away, he couldn't help but notice there wasn't one picture of Money anywhere in sight only pictures of Money's son and Milky.

"So Milky, if you don't mind my asking, what was it like between you and Money?"

"Well Murder, I got pregnant on a humbug and I don't believe in abortions so I kept Lil Money. No, me and your brother were never in a relationship we were just good friends. I mean don't get me wrong he kept us caked up and icy but, we wasn't Fuck buddies. Why you wanna know

Nosey?"

"I'm just tryna see how far I can take this that's all," smiled Murder.

"Oh well, If you driving then I'ma ride or die Chick, I don't want you to fall in love too soon though, you did just come home you might not be ready for this yet. You might need to go get you a six or a seven before you get wit this Dime!" said Milky.

"Girl my name is Murder! And that means I will kill that you heard me?"

"Talk is cheap and bullshit runs a million miles, Lil Money still at school and nobody is in my room right now!" said Milky seductively.

"I ain't scared you lead the way!"

Milky grabbed Murder by his hand and lead him up the stairs and down the hallway to the doorway of the last bedroom. Milky twisted the door knob opening up the way into a sweet smelling but well-kept bedroom. The Queen sized Sealy Posturepedic bed was made up with 3000 count Egyptian cotton sheets and a pink down comforter. There were about 10 goose down pillows spread across the head of the bed. Milky pulled Murder into the room and shut the door. She told him to sit on the edge of the bed while she changed into something more comfortable. Milky turned the 50 inch Plasma TV on, tossed the remote on the bed beside Murder and then sauntered her way into her personal bathroom. Murder smiled to himself as he began to remove his clothing and shoes. *"I couldn't have asked for a better coming home present. Forgive me Big Bro I won't hurt her,"* he thought to himself as he pulled back the comforter and positioned himself between the sheets minus t-shirt and boxers.

Milky stepped out of the bathroom wearing her birthday suit and a pair of 9 inch, Jimmy Cho Stilettos. She blushed as she modeled herself in the bathroom doorway. Just then Murder looked up and instantly felt the blood rush into his manhood. Milky was a sight to behold. Nothing was out of place. She looked as if she worked out every day of the week. If Murder hadn't been lying down he would have had too.

"You like my all natural look?" asked Milky with a smile.

"Baby Girl I thank the Lord that I was blessed with 20/20 vision," said Murder.

Milky smiled teasingly as she slowly strutted towards the bed, "I see you ain't the only one that's glad to see me!" she joked and motioned towards Murders brick hard manhood that had the comforter looking like an Indian Teepee.

"He kinda has a mind of his own but, we share the same tastes in women," said Murder.

"Well I guess I need to thank him for the complement in person!"
Milky pulled back the covers and gasped as she got a close up look at Murder's chiseled and tattooed Caramel brown body. He smirked as he watched her eyes roam over his body and come to a stop on his throbbing hard member. Milky was a giddy as a school girl waiting for the final bell to ring. She quickly kicked off the shoes and positioned herself next to Murder. She cupped Murders chin and turned his face towards her. She then kissed him lightly on his lips. Then a little harder and a little deeper. Her tongue invaded the inside of his mouth and began to intertwine with his. Murder responded to Milky's kiss and began to caress her body with

his finger tips. He pinched, and rolled her nipples, between his index and thumbs this caused a moan to escape from somewhere deep inside of Milky. Milky climbed a top of Murder and began to trail wet kisses from his neck to the tip of his dick. She then used her tongue to circle the head of his manhood before she attempted to take all of him into her mouth. It took a minute to get herself together but, before long Milky had Murder's eyes rolling back in his head and his back in an arch. Murder had his right hand on the back of her head and his left hand gripping the bed spread. Milky sensed Murder's enjoyment and she began to work it over time. At the same time Murder's pleasure was causing her to become wet beyond her wildest dreams. Murder felt ecstasy begin to stir from deep within and he was determined not to explode before he had a chance to lay down his Mack. Murder grabbed Milky around her hips and pulled her above his waist. He smirked when he saw the look on her face.

"Why did you stop me Boy? You couldn't take it huh," she teased.

"You right about that. Ma but, now it's my turn."

Murder rolled Milky onto her back, spread her legs and positioned himself between them. He started with tender kisses on her lips, and then he worked his way down to her breast and on to her erect and hardened nipples. Milky moaned and began to spasm as she came harder than she had in months.

"OH No Miss Thang you don't get off that easy, I'm just beginning," said Murder devilishly.

Before Milky knew what had hit her Murder was tongue deep in her hot, moist, love box. He slowly lapped all around Milky's hardened clitoris before taking it into his mouth and lightly nibbling on it. Milky responded as waves of pleasure began to surge through her body. She grabbed the back of Murder's head and began to grind against his face; in effect she rode his tongue until she began to spasm and wrench in ecstasy again and again. As the last of the orgasms began to subside Murder pushed Milky's legs up and apart. He couldn't stand it any longer. He plunged into Milky with as much restraint as he could muster — Milky gasped as Murder filled her insides to the point of full capacity. It was a feeling that she had almost forgotten.

Murder began to thrust himself deeper and deeper with each stroke. Milky could do nothing but, dig her nails into Murder's back and hang on for the ride. Murder, feeling good about the current outcome of the situation, worked his mid-section with the ferocity and passion of a man on a mission. Once again he felt something start to stir deep inside of him and just as he was about to succumb to this feeling he felt, Milky begin to shake and shudder which caused him to explode in unison wither her. They both had orgasms together and lay intertwined and sweaty in Milky's bed. After catching their breath they sat up and looked each other in the eye and smiled.

"Booooy! I don't know what kinda drug you are but I think I just developed a habit!" said Milky seriously.

"Is that a good thing or a bad thing?" asked Murder.

"I told you I'ma ride or die Chick, so I guess you know that I'm riding with you!"

"That's what I'm talking about Ma! But first we got a lil work to do!"

"Tell me what you need Baby and I'll see what I can do."

"First thing Milk, I need to come up with some Doe so I can get me a click together and get some guns."

"Money won't be a problem Baby. I told you your brother made sure we was good, how much do you need and what the next move?"

"I'm going to need at least 100 grand and then I gotta find some dudes I can trust."

"I'll have the cash for you in the morning and as far as dudes you can trust, I got a few cousins that run a muscle for hire outfit, How's 6 guys sound to you?"

"Perfect Baby Girl, I'm glad you're in my corner you seem to have all the answers."

"Maybe not all the answers but, together we can get to the bottom of this," said Milky.

"The only other thing that I'm going to need is a car."

"No problem Murder your brother's black Audi, A-8 is in the garage, and it's now yours."

"Damn Boo! Why I couldn't have met you before I went to jail?"

"If you had I probably would have been your Girl not Money's baby momma."

"Better late than never, you're my girl now!" said Murder Triumphantly.

"Is that so Mister Man?"

"It sure as hell is now come here and give me some more of that good Shit," laughed Murder as he pulled Milky close.

CHAPTER 23

2 Weeks Later...

Murder had purchased a small arsenal and was getting ready for his afternoon meeting with Milky's cousin Flames and his click known as The Reapers. Flames talked to Murder on the phone and arranged to meet up with him for lunch at Applebee's on Reisterstown Rd. Murder was just finishing up with his shower and Milky had laid out his clothes on the bed.

"Murder, your clothes are on the bed, do you want anything to eat before you leave Baby?

"Nah Ma, I'm taking Flames to lunch so I can meet his boys!"

"Oh OK tell my cousin that I said stop playing bent and call me sometime."

"Aright Boo."

Murder got dressed and made his way downstairs. He stopped in the kitchen to kiss Milky and grab his keys.

"I'm out Baby Girl, I'll call you when I get where I'm going OK?"

"OK Baby, you be careful, oh and here," she said handing him an all-black Walther P89, "don't you ever leave home without it."

"I won't," said Murder before kissing Milky again.

Murder left the house at about 10:30am so that he would have time to scope out the meeting place to make sure it wasn't a set up. He drove across town in silence with only his thoughts to keep him company. First thing he had to do after locking down his new crew was to find out what the streets were saying about Money, find out who he had beef with, and to see who had the most to gain from Money's disappearance.

First things First, he had a meeting to go to so there was no need in jumping the gun. He picked up his Samsung Smart phone and dialed the number he had for Flames.

"Yeah," answered Flames.

"This Murder, I'm on my way don't be late!"

"Oh don't worry, I'm on point you just handle what you need to handle."

"12 on the dot!" said Murder.

"I'll be there."

"One!"

"One!" said Murder before hanging up.

Murder didn't know Flames personally but, he already liked his style and if he was anything like what his cousin told Murder, then he had a new partner and they would be doing big things together.

Murder sat in the driver's seat of his Audi in the parking lot of Applebee's. He had already surveilled the area and was now waiting for Flames to arrive. As he sat and smoked the last of his Newport he noticed an all-black Ford Expedition XL with Limo tinted windows pull into the parking lot. The Ford pulled up in front of the restaurant and dropped off a 6 foot 2 brown skin guy with cornrows. After dropping the man off, the Expedition parked within eyesight of the front door. Murder thought to himself, *"At least he thought to bring backup but, still there's room for improvement. I can teach them a few things."* Murder finished his cigarette before he grabbed his P89 and put it in his waistline. He then rolled up his windows, got out and locked his doors. He walked towards the restaurant door while keeping an eye on the black Ford.

Murder reached the hostess desk she asked was he alone. He replied that he was meeting someone for lunch and gave the fake name that he and Flames picked out earlier. The hostess told Murder to follow her and lead him to a booth in the rear of the restaurant where Flames was already seated.

"I hope you don't mind but, I ordered myself appetizers and a drink," said Flames.

"Nah dawg you cool," said Murder.

"I mean I know you paying but, I was a little hungry."

Murder told the hostess to have the waitress send over another order of appetizers and a rum and coke. Then he seated himself after shaking hands with Flames.

"Where do we start?" asked Murder.

"Your brother, even though I didn't like his relationship with my cousin."

"Well Milky is my problem or should I say blessing now," said Murder defensively.

"Whoa homey Milky's grown and she already filled me in on the situation so don't take offense."

"Aright, let's talk business Flame. How much will it cost me for the muscle that I need to punish whoever is responsible for my brother's demise."

"Well you see homey, I was thinking more along the lines of a brand new partnership between the Reapers and you," said Flames.

"What do you get out of this?"

"We get a 50 percent split of whatever we recover when we do go to war with whoever it is!"

"And?" said Murder.

"And whatever territory we take over, we divide."

"Fair enough, I guess we've got a deal."

Murder and Flames shook hands to seal the deal.

"So now that this is taken care of call the rest of the goons out front and tell them come in so I can meet them."

"OK so Milky ain't lie you on your Shit I see. I like that."

"Don't worry I'm teach y'all every trick I know. My name ain't Murder for nothing!"

"Sounds like a plan to me, let me call these Niggas so we can all get acquainted."

Flames pulled out his Droid Razr and placed a call, 10 minutes later 5 more men were seated with Murder and Flames.

"Murder let me introduce you to the rest of the team."

"OK."

"The short light skinned one to your left is Salty, next to him is Poncho, and to your right is Chubbs and the Twins you see are Keith and Kevin."

"What it do fellas, I'm Murder."

"Yeah we know we heard all about you, you like a legend to us," said Salty.

"I don't know bout no legend but, I'm bout my work," said Murder.

"So, I guess it's time to move on the next step Murder, what we bout to do?" asked Flames.

"Aright I need one of y'all to have his ear to the streets; we need all info the hood has to offer."

"That's easy Poncho got the market cornered on hood rats so I guess he's in charge of intelligence," said Flames.

"Aright Poncho, I need to know what being said about what happened to my brother, who benefited and whatever else sounds like it's worth something," said Murder.

"Sure thing Boss."

"Next we gonna need a few stash houses and safe houses in and around the hood."

"I got this one," said Chubbs.

"Good Chubbs we gonna need 2 stash houses and 3 safe houses," said Murder.

"I'm definitely gonna need some cash to make that happen."

"I got 10 thousand towards that," said Murder.

"Murder we gonna need a way to generate some quick revenue," said Flames.

"That easy Flames, all these so called Lil Hustlers in Baltimore smoke grass right?"

"Yeah don't everybody?"

"Well then, Salty what can you and the Twins do with a couple pounds of Diesel, besides smoke it?"

"Its money over everything Boss," said Salty.

"Yeah just get us the work and we'll get the money," said Keith.

"Aright, last but not least Flame we need 7 boost phones. The old walkie talkie joints and I want you to meet me later on so we can go pick up the grass. As for everybody else we'll meet back up in 2 days to check our progress."

"Aright my Niggas from this point on the Reapers got a job to do and we ain't gonna half-ass. I'll be in contact wit y'all to hand out work phones and to coordinate any of their moves we need to make. Meeting adjourned."

Murder left the restaurant in a good mood. He took 10 thousand out of the trunk and gave it to Chubbs. He gave Flames $1500 for the phones and activation. He called Milky to say he would be home late. Then he started the Audi, lit a Newport and decided to drive through his old hood. As he drove he took notice to how much things had changed and as he pulled onto Harford Rd he began to notice all the new faces posted up on the block. He parked the car and got out to walk into the carry out with the grand opening sign out front.

He grabbed his phone and called Milky to see if she wanted something to eat from the carry out which also gave him a reason to investigate the neighborhood on foot a little bit.

"Hello," said Milky

"Hey Baby, have you eaten yet?

"No but, I am hungry, where are you?"

"I'm on Harford Rd at this new carry out."

"Baby be careful that area use to be your brothers but now I hear there are some treacherous dudes over there."

"Baby I'm strapped and who these dudes suppose to be anyway."

"I don't know their names, just heard something so be on point for me and hurry home."

"OK Babe I will."

Now Murder's interest was peaked. He had to find out more about these so-called gangstas. As trying to place this familiar face in front of him. Once the couple in front of him ordered, Murder stepped up to the register. The cashier asked to take his order but stopped mid-sentence...

"Oh my GOD! What are you doing here?" she asked.

"I'm sorry I know your face but not your name," said Murder.

"Well I know I look a little different because I'm clean now but Murder, I gave you head enough times that I would think you would never forget Joanne Boy!" she said playfully.

"Oh Shit Joanne! Girl you looking real good, how you been?"

"I'm good, when did you get out?"

"Last month."

"I'm sorry bout Money but, Baby Boy this ain't a good place for you to be hanging out."

"I don't want no trouble Joanne, I just want a cheese steak combo and now your number too," smiled Murder.

"I guess I can do that but, Murder you can't be coming around here like that you can get both of us killed, where's your phone?"

Murder handed Joanne his phone so that she could put her number in it. Joanne was an ex-crack head that Murder use to trick off with back in the day when Murder and Money first started to hustle in Northeast. Even though Joanne was caught up in addiction back then, she still looked like something. She dressed in nice clothes, kept a job, and a nice place. Since she wasn't too far gone then, she would go to Murder with whom she had developed a working relationship, and he would trade her drugs for her stunning sexual performances. Murder sat and reminisced while Joanne fixed his order. Neither one took notice of the brown skin dude watching them or the fact that he was listening to their conversation from the last booth on the left.

Smiz was in the middle of his lunch and reading a Chapter of Sun Tzu's, The Art of War when he noticed an unfamiliar man stroll through the front door and start a conversation with the cashier. The man look familiar but, Smiz couldn't make out his face at least until he heard the man's name spoken. Smiz continued to monitor the exchange but, at the same time he pulled his phone and sent a text to 40, alerting him to the situation. After that he waited for instructions and continued to watch.

40 and St. Louis were in their office counting the last of the drop money when 40's iPhone vibrated.

"OK, one of your hood rats is calling," joked St. Louis.

"Man it ain't nobody but your baby momma, I'm let her know you busy right now," said 40 while picking up his phone.

"Oh Shit, St. Louis guess who's back in town?"

"Who? What's her name?"

"Nah Nigga this is business! Serious business."

"Who?

"Remember that Bitch ass Nigga that tried to off my brother?"

"Yeah I remember. What about him?"

"His brother is back in town."

"And? Where is this Nigga? I'll take him to meet his brother!"

"Nah, we gonna see whats with him first, we might not even be a threat but, just in case you know the chic Joanne that works in my carry out?"

"Yeah I know her, she came along way, what's up with her."

"Well Smiz just watched her talking to Murder and she gave him her number, she may be getting ready to give up info she shouldn't repeat."

"You want me to silence her yo?"

"Nah I'm let Smiz earn his cash with this one."

"Good, that Nigga need to do something he getting bored."

"What we gonna do about this Murder cat?"

"Have Raheem follow him and check out his situation."

"I'm on it!"

Smiz's phone vibrated on the table as he sat reading the last of the Chapter in his book. He had carefully watched Joanne put her number into Murder's phone before Murder got his order and left. Now he watched Joanne as she worked and he noticed the confused look on her face. Smiz knew that look well as he had seen it on the faces of his victims. It was the look of contemplation. Joanne was contemplating the betrayal of the one group of people who had seen to it that she was still treated like a person even after years of addiction. Smiz read the text message he received and with a smirk on his face, he gathered the trash and his personal things, and got up to leave. *Time to go to work, Duty Calls*, he thought to himself.

Samir, Raheem, and Black Drew sat in the office of one of their detail shops discussing employees, when Raheem's cell phone went off. He picked it up off the desk and began to read the text message he'd just received from St. Louis.

"Yo fellas head's up. We may have trouble," said Raheem.

"What's wrong Raheem somebody messing with your Peoples?" asked Drew.

"Yeah Slim what got your panties in a bunch?" asked Samir.

"Nah it's way worse than that remember the cat Money?"

"Yeah, he disappeared dummy," said Drew.

"I know that but, his brother just came home and now he asking questions," said Raheem.

"So. That just means he don't know Shit!" said Samir.

"Yeah well 40 and St. Louis said they want me to tail him and find out what I can."

"So what you want us to do?" asked Drew.

"Nothing yet, you and Samir just stay on point cuz I got a feeling Shit bout to get ugly again!"

"Aright Rah, you stay strapped keep ya vest on and your head up, then let us know what's going on."

"You Already!" said Raheem.

Joanne was just finishing the dishes and the rest of the clean up when it hit her. She still had Murder's number and she was itching for some of that! If only for old time sake. She picked up the phone behind the counter and dialed his number. Joanne was so busy on the phone trying to sound sexy she never noticed Smiz creep in through the back door. She continued her conversation as she tried to bait Murder in.

"Yeah Baby Boy I got some info for you but, what you got for me?" she asked seductively.

"What you mean Joanne!" What, you gonna make me give you a couple dollars for it?" asked Murder.

"No Boy! Keep your money. I want something else, if you catch my drift."

"Oh OK well why you ain't say that in the first place Girl."

"Now that we got that established get a pen so you can write down my address Murder."

Smiz made a mental note of Joanne's address and slid out the back door so that he could set up and wait for his unsuspecting victim. He had no feeling on what he was about to do, either way it was work and work equaled money. Joanne finished up her work as she thought about which cute little outfit she would wear, which candles to light, and most importantly which moves from her arsenal she could put on Murder to get him open and checking for her. She turned off the lights and set the alarm before locking the door. She walked out of the alley and down the block. She was so caught up in her thoughts that she never noticed the man dressed in all black at the corner or the fact that all of the street lights were out for the length of the whole block.

Joanne continued up the block towards the bus stop. She toyed with the different scenarios that she could run in her head. There were a few stores that had either just closed or had been closed for a while. She looked at her wrist watch as she passed the 3rd storefront from the corner it was 11:25pm and her bus wasn't due for another 15 minutes. She smiled at the thought of Murder putting his thing down on her. She never noticed the man step out behind her until the hand covered her mouth.

Smiz watched carefully as Joanne walked up the block towards his hiding spot. He had disabled the street lights on the block so that it would be dark. He stood and waited with a brand new straight razor in his right hand. He wore black leather gloves, a black jacket, black jeans, and black Polo boots. Joanne seemed to be lost in thought because as she passed she was smiling. Smiz stepped from the darkened doorway as she passed and he reached around her, covered her mouth and enclosed her in his firm grip so that she could neither run nor scream. He whispered, "Betrayal is the key to the doorway of Death," in her ear. The last thing that Joanne saw or felt was Smiz's gloved right hand slide from the base of her left ear the base of her right ear. At First she thought maybe he was smearing something on her skin. Then it became harder to breath and she felt dizzy. She touched a tickle on her neck with her hands and when she looked at her hands the sickening sight of dark burgundy was all she saw. Then she fell to the ground and tried to scream. The only sound that could be heard was gurgling and retreating footsteps.

Smiz took out his phone and sent two texts. One text went to 40 letting him know that the job was done. The other went to Raheem letting him know that Murder would be at this address at 11:45pm and that he would be able to follow him from the address to wherever he was staying. He then closed the phone and disappeared until his services were needed again. Murder was just leaving the weed spot that he had set up. Salty and the Twins were moving jars and quarters of the Sour Diesel like it was going out of style. At the rate that Salty and the Twins moved the weed. Their money would be up to par in no time. Chubbs called earlier with the locations of the stash houses and the locations of the safe houses. He told Murder that he would get keys made the morning. Poncho checked in, he was doing the hood rat thing and digging for info. He too said that he would check in tomorrow. Flames was there with Murder making sure everything was running right.

"So far so good, Huh? Murder," said Flames.

"What can I say? You Niggas is men of y'all word."

"Money over everything and loyalty over Bitches, dawg."

"I agree whole hardheartedly!" said Murder.

"So what's the plans for tomorrow?"

"I need you to pick up the guns in the am. Make sure everybody stay strapped and ready. I got something to, go check on tonight but, I'll hit you in the morning."

"Aright that's whassup."

Murder jumped in the Audi stashed the P-89, and lit a cigarette. He pulled out his phone called Milky, looked at the address for Joanne and drove to her apartment in South Baltimore's Brooklyn Homes.

Raheem was just busting a nut in the Magnum that was buried deep inside his lil hood rat fling when his phone chirped, "Ooh Daddy I love it when you hit from the back like that!" cooed Nikki.

"Girl you love it when I do it anyway that I do it! Now get up and make me a sandwich."

"OK Baby, what you want on it?"

"Some of that Smoked Turkey, Chicken Breast, Provolone Cheese, Mayo, and Mustard! Oh yeah some Doritos and a Cold Nestle."

"OK Baby, Here, your phone going off," said Nikki.

"Let me see that with ya Nosey Ass, It ain't no Bitches so go get my food."

"It better not be!"

"Bitch! Go get my Food before you make me act ugly in this Motherfucker. That's your problem, you don't know how to quit while you ahead!" yelled Raheem.

"I'm sorry Daddy, I ain't mean anything by that."

"Go do what I told you!"

Raheem looked at the phone and read the message. He checked the time and then got up to go wash is nuts. He had work to do so Nikki would have to wait. Pussy was good but his team was his life. 10 minutes later Raheem was dressed and grabbed his sandwich, Doritos, and Nestle.

"I'll be back in a few so keep it warm."

"OK Daddy don't be long."

Murder sat in the Audi on 9th Street smoking a cigarette and checking the time. It was 12:15am and Joanne still hadn't shown up or called. He got out and was about to go and knock on the door. He stepped off the curb looking up at the bedroom window and was almost hit by a dude in a black SUV. He apologized and waited as the truck passed. Murder was so preoccupied with the whereabouts of Joanne that he paid no attention to the truck or the driver so he never saw the truck U-turn and park at the end of the block.

Raheem was so busy looking for the track featuring Neo on Young Jeezy's TM-103 that he didn't see Murder step off the curb and into the path of the black Porsche truck. He almost ran him over so he ended up slamming on brakes and blowing the horn.

He could see that the man was per-occupied with something else and was glad he made no eye contact. After the near miss, Raheem drove to the end of the block made a U-turn and parked at the bottom of 9th Street and watched Murder knock on the door repeatedly and got no answer. After about 15 more minutes. Murder started his Audi and pulled out of his parking space. Raheem eased out his space and began to follow Murder without being spotted.

Murder was upset because he thought that Joanne was playing games with him. He made a mental note to stop past her job and curse her ass out but for now he knew he had to get home to Milky and Lil Money. They had become quite the little family and Murder felt that this was something he had been missing in his life.

Raheem continued to follow Murder until they ended up in Woodlawn. He watched as Murder pulled into the driveway of a house and wrote down the address. He decided that he would check and see whose name the house was in and he wrote down the tag numbers on the Audi and the truck so that Nikki could check the registrations when he dropped her off at her job with Department of Motor Vehicles tomorrow. As for now, he had pussy on pause and he was headed back to it, 40 and St. Louis would get a report in the morning.

The next morning, Milky and Murder laid cuddled up after their early morning love session. They got started as soon as the school bus deported with Lil Money on it.

"Damn Babe, that's the way that a man should wake up Every Day!" say Murder.

"Shit! That's the way a woman should be awaken Boo," giggled Milky.

"Turn on the TV Babe. I wanna catch the news."

"Speaking of news, have you heard anything from the streets?"

"I thought I had something with this girl named Joanne but, she never showed up."

"Whoa! Who is Joanne?"

"It's nothing like that Milky she's just a chic that me and Money use to sell crack to back in the day. She's clean now and working over in East Baltimore. She was suppose to give me some inside info last night but she never showed up!"

"So that's where you were last night huh?"

"Baby don't look at me like that. It was business now can you please turn on the news?"

"Yeah OK, It better be business."

Milky turned the flat screen on to the local morning news show. Don Scott and Marty Bass were just going over local news stories when one particular name jumped out at Murder. Marty Bass was saying something about a Joanne Jackson whose body was discovered about a block from her place of employment. She was found fully dressed with her throat slit. Robbery wasn't a motive, neither was rape. Murder couldn't believe what he was seeing and hearing. Could it be a coincidence or was this the result of someone trying to keep her quiet.

"Baby, that wasn't the girl you were suppose to meet with last night, was it?"

"Yeah it looks that way Baby."

"Man if these dudes did that to her for attempting to meet with you, then you better be careful!"

"I don't know what's what yet Boo don't start worrying OK."

"OK, Baby!"

"I gotta call Flames, hand me my phone."

It was 9am but 40 and St. Louis had been up and moving since 7am. Raheem had called and give the address to the house and let 40 know that Nikki was on her job and going to get the info on the registrations for the car and trunk. Smiz didn't have to call in, his work was all over the television but, it wouldn't come back on the Wild Boyz. Samir and Black Drew were at the auto shop waiting on the next move.

St. Louis you still got that computer geek chic?"

"Yeah I was just with Tia, why you need her to run the address on the house?"

"Yeah get her on that while I figure out the next move."

"Aright that's whassup!"

Act II

The Next Week...

Murder and Flames were sitting in the upstairs back bedroom of one of their safe houses counting up the money from the weed spot. The rest of the Reapers were present because it was time for the weekly meeting.

"Flames, where do we stand with the guns, and stash?" asked Murder.

"We got enough weed to last out the rest of this month, as far as guns we got 10 assault rifles, 20 hand guns, 7 vest's," said Flames.

"Good! Poncho what Intel do you have for us?"

"Well first off, the thing with this Joanne chick. Nobody knows who did it, but, it was definitely a hit. I didn't think it was relevant to us until I found out who she worked for."

"And who is that?" asked Flames and Murder.

"Check me out. This Shit is gonna kill two birds with one stone!" said Poncho.

"Spit it out Nigga we ain't got all Fucking day!" said Murder heatedly.

"Y'all ever heard of the Wild Boyz?"

"Ain't they the crew that's running the lower East Side?" asked Chubbs.

"Yeah it would seem that they swallowed up all the territory that Money had."

"OK and that relates to us how?" asked Murder.

"I'm getting to it Boss!"

"Well hurry the Fuck up Dummy," said Flames.

"It seems as though Money was the target of a botched hit by some dudes called C-4, but nobody knows what really happened to C-4 or what actually happened to Money!”

"So I say again how does that relate to us!?" asked Murder again!

"Wasn't C-4 the suspects in that FBI case not too long ago? You know the one where the dude and his girl was hitting dudes and got themselves killed?" said Keith.

"Yeah only I happen to know that there was one more member of C-4 that disappeared," said Kevin!

"What you mean by disappeared?" asked Murder.

"Just that," said Poncho, clearing irritated.

"The dudes name was Cash; and his right hand man was a cat name FO-Pound. He's the one who got killed along with his girl."

"Who killed them?" said Flames

"That's where I was headed. They were killed by Money's goons."

"How do you know that?" asked Murder.

"Because one of Money's goons was killed at the scene of that crime."

"And this happened before my brother disappeared?" asked Murder.

"As far as I can tell yes!"

"So where did Cash disappear too?

"No one knows Boss."

"So how the Fuck does that help us!?" screamed Murder as he banged on the table.

"Well boss, Cash had a brother! He's the head of the Wild Boyz and his name is 40. Guess who Joanne worked for?"

"Well I'll be damned. I guess you are good for something after all," said Flames.

"So what's the next move Boss?" said Poncho.

"See what you can find out about these Wild Boyz but don't make any noise! At least not yet, just do your home Work. The rest of y'all concentrate on your everyday hustles. We gotta stack doe and get ready. I got a feeling we about to go to war!" said Murder.

40 picked up this throw away cell phone and dialed a number with a 404 area code and waited as the phone rang.

"What up douche bag?" said Cash.

"Fuck you too Cock boy," said 40 "what's good?"

"Not a lot but, I thought I'd keep you posted!"

"Posted about what?"

"Well it seems that trash that we took out has been recycled."

"What? When did he show face?"

"Last month but, I got this!"

"If you need me I'm Here!"

"I said I got this Bro."

"OK but at least fill me in on what you know!"

"Right now all I know is that he's asking questions and he's Fucking his brother's baby momma!"

"It figures!"

"Anyway how are Reecy and the twins?"

"Everybody's cool."

"Good! Look if it gets hot here I'm sending guards in on the covert!"

"Boy I'm good, I got me and my family, you just stay on point!"

"I meant what I said, so it's not up for debate. I'll keep you posted!"

"One!"

"One!"

St. Louis walked into the room just as 40 was getting off the phone.

"Raheem's Shorty confirmed that both vehicles are in the same name as the house. Milkeena Steward, Money's baby momma."

"So what's next?" asked St. Louis.

"I got Samir watching the house right now and Drew is following up on some leads in the street."

"Yeah I heard that Murder is running with some dudes called the Reapers. They opened a weed spot and they taking down a little bit."

"Now that, I didn't know. Put everyone on alert it may be war time soon."

Over the next two weeks, the two teams played cat and mouse trying to collect any and all info on each other that they could. Samir continued to watch Milky's and Murder's schedules down pat. Murder found out the locations to two more of the Wild Boyz legitimate businesses' but wasn't able to pin point the movements of 40 or his right hand St. Louis. The Reapers were getting irritated and were ready to make some noise. A few of the hot heads began to plot without Murder or Flames knowing. Salty, Keith, and Kevin sat in the half empty row house on Fulton Ave in West Baltimore, smoking on 2 blunts and sipping on a 5th of Ciroc Vodka.

"Yo I don't know about y'all Niggas but, I'm ready to make some moves. Murder must have gotten soft from his time in the pen!" said Salty between pulls on the blunt.

"Yeah I'm feeling that Salty. We need to do something and fast!" said

Kevin.

"I got something that will get these punk-ass Wild Boyz attention, plus it'll hurt they pockets," said Keith.

"Oh yeah whats that?" said Salty.

"I say we hit their carry out on Harford Rd, take the cash, shoot it up, and make them Niggas make a move!" said Keith.

"Sounds cool but, we gotta do it smart," said Salty.

"All we gotta do is mask up, pull it off, then bounce. Flames and Murder won't know who hit what and the best part is we get to keep the cash!"

"I say we wait till after the lunch rush and hit them so we know the cash is there!" said Salty.

"It's a plan then tomorrow at 2:30pm," said Keith.

"That's what it is!" said Kevin.

The next morning 40 sat in his office upstairs from the carry out. He was waiting for St. Louis, Raheem, and Drew, so that they could come up with a plan to handle The Reapers and Murder. Smiz was still on standby and Samir was stilling watching Milky's house. About 1:00pm Raheem made his way to the office and sat down to tell 40 that he had discovered that Milky was related to the head of the Reapers. At about 2:00pm Drew dragged himself in arguing with his girlfriend on the phone. St. Louis called and said that he would be there in 20-25 minutes. After Drew finished his phone call Raheem and 40 brought him up to speed on the situation. At 2:25pm Raheem and Drew went downstairs into the carry out to order lunch. They took a seat in the very last booth on the right. As the waitress brought their orders, St. Louis walked into the carry out.

"What it do my Niggs?" asked St. Louis while facing a seat across from Raheem.

"Shit chilling bout to get my eat on," said Raheem.

"The only thing on my mind is these clowns that asking questions bout us but, as always I'm ready!" said Drew.

"I feel you dawg, I stay strapped and ready," joked St Louis.

As they sat and joked Raheem caught movement out the corner of his eye and tapped St. Louis and Drew.

"Three Niggas in mask coming in the front door get ready but, don't move yet," said Raheem as he drew his Desert Eagle 50 caliber.

Drew pulled his Sig Sauer 45, and St. Louis pulled his Glock 357. The 3 figures burst through the front door brandishing 2 Pump shotguns, and a Tech-9. Keith waited by the front door to block any escape, Salty hopped the counter and ran to the manager's office; Kevin went to empty the cash registers. All three were so high and jacked up off of adrenaline that neither one noticed the three men that sprang from the last booth. Keith had his back turned when Raheem squeezed off four 50 caliber rounds that hit Keith in his back head and neck. He was dead before his faceless body slumped to the floor. Kevin saw his brother's demise but, before he could aim three 45 slugs tore into his chest shredding his heart and collapsing his lungs. A last minute muscle spasm caused him to squeeze the trigger and spray buck shot from the 12 gauge and hit Drew's left arm. St. Louis was on his way to the manager's office but Salty had heard the gun shots and had already hit the back door and was running down the alley.

40 heard the commotion upstairs and had already put a plan into action the money was put up and it was time to evacuate his men. The police were on the way along with an ambulance for Drew. Raheem and St. Louis had to leave but Drew would have to wait. The gun that he used was registered to him and he was on record as Store Security. Once he entered the restaurant he immediately took over the scene and waited for the authorities.

Salty sat in the driver seat of the tinted out hooptie as close to crying as he had been in years. They had Fucked up and now the Twins were dead. There was going to be hell to pay, and it was all his fault. He made up his mind right there that he would go to the stash house take the cash and get lost.

The police had processed the scene, bagged the bodies, and detained Drew at the hospital until they could investigate the attempted robbery. They told 40 that it wouldn't be a problem since the two masked gun men were already wanted on robbery and weapons charges. St. Louis and Raheem were at the office in the detail shop awaiting 40's arrival. 40 managed to obtain the names of the Twins and had already had a source determine that they were Reapers.

"So Murder you want to war, I'm show you how," said 40 to no one in particular.

40 locked up the carry out grabbed up his twin Glock 19's, jumped in his armored S-Class and called Smiz.

"Yo!" said Smiz

"Meet me at the car shop."

"I'm 15 minutes out."

"One!"

"One!"

Murder and Flames sat in the safe house frustrated because they could not contact Salty, Keith, or Kevin. Chubbs and Poncho were on their way to the house but Murder was heated.

"Flames, I hope these Niggas ain't somewhere Flickin off!" said Murder.

"If they are don't worry I'm be the one to deal with them," said Flames.

"You found out anything new on these Wild Boyz Nigga?"

"Nah but, it won't be long."

Just then Murder's cell phone chirped with a text message from Milky, It read: *turn on the television quick. It seems somebody beat you to the punch.* He read the text message to Flames, who only could guess what it meant, Murder turned on the new and saw the front doors of the carry out blocked off with yellow tape and the Head Line read: *Two Dead, One Wounded in botched robbery attempt.* Murder had a sick feeling in the pit of his stomach and they began to call Salty and the Twins again.

Salty parked the hooptie in the alley and went in through the backdoor. He made a beeline for the safe with a small black duffel bag. His phone continued to vibrate but, he would never answer it. He opened the safe and put all the money and the 3 remaining pounds of Sour Diesel in the bag. He took the bag back to the car and put it in the back seat. He grabbed two 5 gallon gas cans from the trunk and damn near jumped out of his skin when he notice a passed out dope fiend slumped in a high stupor on the basement steps. That gave him an idea. He sat the gas cans inside the backdoor and turned towards the dirty fiend,

"Ay Unc you busy?" he asked.

The fiend jumped as the voice woke him from his nod, "Nah Nephew what you need?"

"I just bought 20 grams of raw and I need somebody to test it for me."

"OH in that case then I'm your man!"

"Come on in Unc."

The dope fiend got up and walked past Salty into the kitchen. As soon as he passed Salty, he stood in the middle of the floor and greedily waited for his dope. Salty pulled a snub nosed 38 and shot the fiend in the back of his head twice. He then doused the place and the body with gasoline and lit the fire before hopping in the car and heading for 95 South.

40 finally made it to the detail shop and everyone was there except for Drew, who was at the hospital, and Samir, who was still watching Milky's. Samir was there on a conference call.

"What the Fuck just happened?" asked Samir.

"Three of them Reaper Niggas tried to hit either the carry out or us," said Raheem.

"Shit if it wasn't for Raheem's sharp eye they probably would have succeeded," said St. Louis.

"Something wasn't right about that whole move but, I ain't got time to figure it out now."

"Where's Smiz?" said 40.

"Over here!" said Smiz which caused everybody to jump and pull pistols.

"MOTHAFUCKA! How the hell do you do that Shit?" said St. Louis.

"Years of practice my Brother," said Smiz.

"OK here is the plan, Smiz you and Samir go get his girl and baby and take them to one of our safe houses. Blindfold them but, don't hurt them!"

"Samir I'm on my way!" said Smiz.

"Call me when you're close."

"Will do!" said Smiz.

"Raheem, go find out all the locations to the Repeater strong holds."

"Got it."

"St. Louis go and get the war toys ready!"

"We'll meet back here tomorrow night but, be careful because Murder is gonna be upset that his Bitch is gone!"

"One!"

"One!"

Murder's phone went off again as Chubbs walked in the room. They still hadn't heard from Salty or the Twins either.

"Hello!" said Murder.

"Boss you ain't gonna believe or like the news that I got for you!" said Poncho.

"Just spit it the Fuck out!"

"Well I got info saying that... that was the Twins that got bodied at that carry out," said Poncho.

"What the Fuck? Are you sure?"

"95%, I'm still checking into it, but that's not all, it gets worse!"

"How much worse?"

"I just drove down the block and the weed spot is burning to the ground!"

"The what?"

"The weed spot is being put out as we speak by the Fire Department."

"Mothafucker!!! Poncho hurry up and get back here!"

"What was all that?" asked Flames.

"The Twins are dead and the weed spot is burning up as we speak."

"What?"

"Where the Fuck is Salty?"

"Nobody knows."

"Chubbs do you still Fuck with that chick Nikki that works at the DMV?" asked Flames.

"We still cool, why what you need?"

"First we need to find out the license plate numbers on these Wild Boyz Clowns cars then we can get some addresses."

"I'ma call her in a few and see what's up."

"Aright we gonna lay low and see what's what, I want everybody here until we know what's good."

"Chubbs call Shorty then go get her and get to work," said Flames.

"Aright."

Samir was parked across the street on the side block when Smiz hit his phone and said he was there. Before Samir could grab his gun and get out Smiz opened the passenger side door and got in.

"What up Bro?" said Smiz causing Samir to jump.

"Why the Fuck do you always do that Nigga?"

"My bad get your ass on point Then!"

"Anyway how we gonna do this?"

"Right now she should be in the kitchen cooking. Its 6pm so all we gotta do is go in grab them and leave."

"Let me handle the going in, you just pull the truck up front," said Smiz.

"It's your world, I'm just a squirrel, let's do this!"

Smiz got out of the truck, walked across the street and disappeared up the block. Samir started his truck and eased out of the parking space. As he pulled into the drive of the house he noticed that all of the electricity instantly went off.

"Mommy I'm scared!" said Lil Money.

"Don't worry Baby it's just the circuit breakers. I'll go out to the garage and reset them," said Milky.

"Mommy don't go out there! I just saw the boogie man!"

"Boy you ain't watching any more late night movies. Ain't no such thing as that!"

No sooner than Milky said the words a gloved hand covered her mouth and the barrel of a pistol pressed into her back.

"You should learn to listen to children. Their eyes do not lie and their thoughts are pure," Smiz whispered into her ear.

Samir sat in the truck and kept an eye on the street for any movement. When the front door jerked open it startled him to see two duct taped people followed by Smiz. He hopped out and ran around to open the back door. He took notice of the terrified looks on the faces of Milky and Lil Money before he reached in and put the hoods over their heads.

"Forget what you saw, cooperate and both of y'all will live," said Samir.

Smiz only laughed at what was said and then he jumped into the passenger seat and closed the door. He texted the mission accomplished message to 40 and St. Louis. Samir jumped in, started the truck, and took their prisoner's across town to another of the Wild Boyz safe houses. Upon arrival Smiz and Samir settled in to waiting for the next assignment.

Nikki's cell phone rang just as she finished drying off from her shower. She picked it up and hesitated before answering... *What the Fuck his fat ass want?"* she thought.

"Hello said Nikki.

"What's up Ma? Longtime no hear from. How you been?"

"I'm good. Where have you been Stranger?"

"You know here there and taking care of B.I."

"So what's up?"

"Truthfully Baby Girl I need a favor."

"OK shoot."

"You still work down the DMV?"

"Yeah Why?"

"I need some info on some dudes."

"What dudes?"

"You ever heard of some dudes call the Wild Boyz?"

At that point Nikki's heart began to beat faster but, she could let on that she knew anything, "Never heard of them. Who are they?"

"Don't worry bout it then, look I'ma call you back with the tag number and a Lil Cash for you but, you gonna owe me a date! Cool?"

"You got that Baby. I'll ask some of my girlfriends and see what I can find out about these Wild Ones or Wild Boyz and call you back... Okay Boo?"

No sooner than she hung up with Chubbs she called Raheem and explained the phone call that she had just received. Raheem told her not to worry he would handle everything and for her to play along with Chubbs until he got back with her. Raheem called 40 to let him know what had just happened and to explain the plan that he had just come up with. Come tomorrow it would be their turn to strike back.

Chubb's hung up his phone and smiled, at least he would come through with his assignment he thought. He walked back into the room and waited for Murder to get off of his phone before he spoke.

Murder put down the phone and with a frustrated look on his face he asked, "What's good, Chubbs?"

"I just got off the phone with that Shorty and everything is a go, she even said she gonna see if she can find out anything on her own. You know them hood rats rosy as Shit!"

"GOOD, GOOD. Chubbs go ahead home we'll meet back here in the morning."

"OK Boss!" said Chubbs before getting up to leave.

Murder turned to Flames and said, "I can't get Milky on the phone. I hope the Twins didn't put her in harm's way with their dumb ass move, and where the Fuck is Salty?"

"She's probably just sleep Murder its late maybe you should get home to your family and let me worry about Salty!"

"Yeah maybe you right my Nigga, call me when you find out. It don't matter what time it is."

"Aright," said Flame as Murder and he got up to leave.

40 and St. Louis had just finished listening to Raheem's plan and were about to leave the shop to go to the safe house were Milky and Lil Money were stashed.

"40 we should get a good night's sleep because come the morning, we gonna be at war!" said St.

"Yeah I know but I just wanna see what this broad knows before the Shit hits the fan."

Murder couldn't concentrate as he drove to his house. He called Milky's phone back to back without an answer. He tried the house phone and still got no answer. At that point he began to drive as fast as the City streets allowed him. He was interrupted from his thoughts when Poncho called his phone to tell him that once the Fire Department had put out the flames a body was found in the kitchen but, it had not been identified yet.

Murder pulled into the driveway as soon as he hung up with Poncho. He saw Milky's truck in the driveway but once he realized the front door was open; his heart began to pound ferociously. He jumped out of the driver's seat and ran to the door yelling out Milky's name. He received no answer.

Murder drew is pistol and began to search the house.

After searching high and low to no avail, Murder called Flames and told him what had happened.

"Flames where the Fuck are you?" asked Murder.

"Shit Murder, I just laid my ass down, whassup?"

"They took Milky and Lil Money," said Murder as close to tears as he had ever been. Flames was caught off guard at the words that came out of Murder's mouth.

"Whoa! Who took my cousin and her kid?"

"I don't know! The only Niggas I can think of is them Wild Boyz Niggas."

"You sure she ain't with one of her friends or something?"

"Man I've been calling her since we was at the safe house."

"FUCK, FUCK, FUCK! What's the next move?"

"All I'm gonna do is wait here and see if they contact me, but you call up the rest of the crew. Tell them to get ready for war, and have Chubbs get on his job first thing in the morning!"

"You gonna be aright tonight?

"Yeah I'm good, you just make sure we don't have no more Fuck ups, because the Twins cause this Shit!"

"Aright Murder, I'm on it, One!"

"One!"

40 and St. Louis pulled up to a 2 story Victorian house in the Liberty Heights section of Northwest Baltimore. It was 11:45pm but time seemed to be standing still. 40 and St. Louis went around to the back and entered

through the basement door.

Raheem pulled up in front of Nikki apartment building and called her phone.

"Baby, you ready? I'm downstairs!

"I'm on my way down Raheem gimme a sec!"

Five minutes later Nikki came out the door dressed in a pair of skin tight Rock and Republic jeans and a Roca Wear jacket. She opened the door, hopped in, and kissed Raheem.

"Did that dude call you back?"

"Not yet Boo!"

"Aright well we going to my house and then you can call him and give him this info that I made up. Then after that I can give you this thing I got for you!"

Raheem smiled at Nikki and blew her a kiss.

"OOH Daddy, you promise?" Nikki cooed.

"Business First, Pleasure after!"

"Okay Let's Go!"

40, Samir, Smiz and St. Louis stood in a semi-circle around the chair where a blind folded, hooded and duct taped Milky sat nervously crying.

"Look Baby Girl, this ain't about you, so if you want to walk away unharmed you'll help us out!" said 40.

"Help you do what? Who are you? And what do you want?" Milky cried.

"Bitch don't worry about who we are, If you love that Lil Nigga over there you better tell us who that Nigga Murder is running with and why he shot up an innocent carry out!" said St. Louis.

"Oh My God! Please don't hurt my child! I didn't know nothing about no carry out."

"Man this Bitch putting on a good act but, let's see if she still got amnesia once I cut this Lil Niggas fingers off!" said Smiz.

"Noooooo! Okay, okay he rolling with my cousin, Flames and his crew but, I swear to you I don't know where they hang out, please don't hurt us.

"Aright Baby Girl, we ain't into hurting women and kids unless we gotta so as long as what you say checks out, we gonna let you go unharmed, Okay!"

40 already knew that Milky had told the truth because he knew about the Reapers. He really just wanted Milky and her son out of the way when the bullets started to fly, plus he knew that as long as he had the girl and her son he had Murder's head. 40 told Samir to stay downstairs and take care of the prisoners. Everyone else went upstairs to plan for tomorrow.

"Alright fellas here's the plan, Smiz get with Raheem because you and him are going to take out the rest of the Reapers, He'll explain!" said 40.

"St. Louis you go get the war toys and bring them here, we'll stage up here, any questions?"

"What you gonna do Boss?" asked St. Louis.

"Me I'ma put together the rest of the plan so that once it's over we come out clean and keep it moving. Plus, I gotta take care of Drew. Then, I have a phone call to make!"

"Aright."

Chubb's phone rang and woke him from his sleep. He glanced at the clock on his night stand and it read 1:20am.

"Who the Fuck? Hello," said Chubbs.

"Hey Chubbs this is Nikki, I'm sorry to call you so late, but, I just couldn't wait to give you the info that I found out!"

"Don't sweat it, Baby Girl. You did good what you got for me?"

"Well, me and my girls couldn't find out the tag numbers but, we did find out the addresses to three of their stash houses."

"Damn Boo how did y'all pull that off?"

"The power of the P-U-S-S-Y Boy!" laughed Nikki.

"Aright hold on let me get myself a pen and paper."

"OK!"

"Aright Baby I'm back."

"You ready?"

"Yeah."

"OK."

By the time Chubbs finished writing down all the info he had promised to drop some money off to Nikki, by tomorrow afternoon. Raheem explained the plan to Smiz and agreed to meet up at the Liberty Heights house by 7am so that they could put their plan in motion. He noticed the look that Nikki was giving him as he hung up.

"And now Mr. Man its time you make good on your promise!"

"Gladly Miss Thang, now kindly get Naked! Please!"

Murder couldn't sleep so he sat in the living room recliner with the phone in one hand and a pistol in the other. His mind was racing as he wondered about the safety of Milky and Lil Money. He bounced back and forth between anger at the stupidity of the Twins, sadness at what happened to Milky, and thought of Revenge against the Wild Boyz. While Murder was lost in his thoughts his phone rang.

He looked at it and saw that the number of the incoming call was restricted.

"Hello!"

"Don't say Nothing! Just Listen!" said the slightly muffled voice.

"We have your Bitch and her brat. All you have to do to get them back is come up with $100,000 cash. We will call you back with instructions!"

Then the phone went dead.

"Hello! Hello! Noooooo!"

The sun was starting to rise by the time Murder got a hold of Flames. He told Flames about the phone call and Flames told him about the info that he got from Chubbs. Poncho had also called to say that the body recovered from the fire wasn't Salty.

"Aright Flames this what I want done, First we gonna need a few more goons that we can trust to follow orders. No Hot Heads!"

"OK."

"Then get everybody together and ready because to hit these three addresses. You head up to one, Poncho to one, and Chubbs to one."

"Who' going with you to make the drop?"

"If y'all ain't finish I'm going alone but, I got something for these dudes, I'ma make a drop alright!"

By 9am, Smiz and Raheem had all of their traps set and ready to spring. 40 and St. Louis were out making sure everything else was in order and Samir was tending to his prisoners.

"You need to go to the bathroom Shorty," said Samir.

"Please Mister I promise I won't try anything."

"Shit! Why me? Aright hold up."

Samir put down his pistol on the table and walked over to the chair where Milky was taped and hooded. He leaned over her and removed her hood and blind fold; next he cut the tape binding her wrists. Once he had taken the blind fold and hood off, Milky sat still until her eyes adjusted to the light. When her eyes focused she quickly looked around the room for Lil Money but didn't see him. What she did see was a big black semi-automatic hand gun on the table about 5 feet from where she was sitting. In the back of her mind she thought, *"My son, and I have to get out of here! Murder where are you?"*

She was snapped out of her thoughts when Samir spoke, "Aright get up and don't try nothing funny."

"I won't."

Milky stood on shaky legs and started towards the door. Samir sneezed and in that instance Milky darted for the table and grabbed the pistol. Samir recover from the sneeze, realized what was happening and gave chase but it was already too late. By the time that Samir lunged toward Milky she spun around, faced Samir and fired 3 shots into his chest. Samir caught the 3 impacts to his chest and flipped over the chair landing face down on the floor.

Milky tossed the still smoking pistol onto the table and ran out the door, she began to scream, "Money! Money! Where are you Baby?" As she moved through the hallway almost at a panic, she made her way to the stairs and up to the first floor. She called out to her son once more and then she heard a muffled sound coming from a room off to the left. She ran to the door and pushed it open. Lil Money was duck taped to the chair, blind folded and hooded as she was.

Milky walk over to the chair but, before she could begin to undo the tape that held her son. She felt a sharp pain from a blow to the back of her head and the last thing she saw before she lost consciousness was the sneering face of Samir. "Stupid ass Bitch you should have aimed a little higher!"

"Flames came up with 6 more goons too make up 3 teams of 3. Poncho and Chubbs each along with Flames made sure that their teams were armed and ready. Murder came in with a frustrated look on his face.

"Aright Flames you and your team will take the West Baltimore address, Chubbs you and your team take the South Baltimore address and Poncho, y'all do the County address."

"Aright Murder but you be careful and watch out for them dudes," said Flames.

Smiz and Raheem were just finishing the trap at the County House when they noticed a blue Chevy Caprice pull slowly into the block.

"Heads up," said Raheem.

"I'm already on it, get ready," said Smiz before ducking off into the bushes. Poncho and his two goons eyeballed the address before pulling into a parking space in front of the house. They checked their weapons and exited the vehicles heading straight for the front porch.

"One of y'all take the back door the other one come with me!"

The brown skin goon started around the side of the house but, as soon as he passed the bushes Smiz stepped out behind him and plunged a switchblade into the base of his skull causing him to die a violent and instant death. Smiz then placed the body in a slumped position against the house. Raheem was already in his SUV with engine idling awaiting Smiz. He caught movement in his rear view mirror and knew that it was Smiz. Smiz slid into the passenger seat with a detonator in his left hand and an evil smirk on his face.

"As soon as they kick the door in I push this button. Then we get to go and have some more fun."

Poncho was eager to get some REC so he brazenly kicked the door to the house off the hinges.

"Fuck you Niggas!" he yelled as he and the goon rushed in spraying bullets at everything in sight. They continued to shoot through every door and wall in sight.

Raheem was watching intently from across the street when he noticed the action.

"It's game time Smiz push the button!"

"I'm on it already."

Raheem's black SUV was pulling out of the parking space when the first explosion ripped through the basement floor causing the house to collapse on top of itself.

"One down two to go," said Smiz."

"You sure that the South Baltimore house will detonate without us there?"

"Trust me I do this for a living just hurry up and get us to West Baltimore because this one is gonna be hands on."

"I'm always down for some wet work," said Raheem.

40 and St. Louis arrived at the safe house and when they entered all they heard was Samir cussing like a sailor. They could smell the acrid smell of gun powder hanging in the air.

"What the Fuck is going on in here?" asked 40 as he and St. Louis descended the steps into the basement.

"Yeah Samir why it smell like somebody been busting guns all up in here?" asked St. Louis.

"Man this dumb ass Bitch shot me 3 times in my vest and tried to escape so I ended up having to crack her in the back of her head!"

"Please tell you ain't Kill her!" said 40.

"Nah, I just knocked her brains loose that all," snickered Samir.

"What about the kid?" asked St. Louis.

"He still OK. Just scared out of his mind," said Samir.

"Aright, y'all take care of them two. I got a phone call to make."

Murder sat awaiting the phone call. He was nervous as Shit but he knew that he had to keep his head on straight. He wondered how things were going with Flames, Poncho, and Chubbs. No matter, it would, it would all be over soon then he and Milky could move on with their lives and try to become something more. First he had to finish what he had started, if not his revenge would eat him alive. Murder was startled out of his revelry by his phone ringing...

Meanwhile, Chubbs and his three man team pulled up to a house in the Pig Town section of South Baltimore. Chubbs' plan was to hit the house fast and hard. All three were to bum rush the front door and shoot any and everyone in sight. After double parking their vehicle in front of the house, they all checked and double checked their weapons and body armor before they exited.

"This is it Boys, shoot to Kill and don't let anyone or anything live! We gonna get it and get out. Shit I got some pussy waiting for me after this," said Chubbs.

Little did they know that the vacant house that they were about to enter had been constantly filling with natural gas, from a huge hole in the supply pipe, since 7am this morning.

Chubbs and his team moved with purpose as they had gotten out of the vehicle, unknown to them they were living on borrowed time.

As they stood on the steps one of the goons kicked the door causing the hinges to splinter and the door to cave in ward. Then they all rushed inside and started shooting. Chubbs caught the rotten egg stench of natural gas but before he could give the order to cease fire the gas ignited from the muzzle flashes of the assault rifles. The last thing that any one felt was the heat from the flash fire that instantly burned all three bodies beyond recognition.

The voice at the other end of the phone told Murder that he was to bring the 100 Grand to the Owings Mills Metro/Subway parking lot where someone would be waiting in a mini-van to pick it up.

Once he had given the money to the driver, the driver would then give him a piece of paper with the address where he could pick up Milky. After relaying the instructions to Murder, 40 hung up abruptly.

40 turned to St. Louis and said, "Get one of our throwaway minivans with the Limo tint on it and put a duffel bag with 4 bricks in it in the passenger seat!!"

"What's that for?" said St. Louis.

"OH Don't Worry I got a plan that's gonna kill two birds with one stone," smirked 40.

"What about the kid?" asked Samir.

"You put the kid in your car and drive him to Virginia somewhere and release him on some church steps or at a hospital or something."

Smiz and Raheem made it to the house in West Baltimore with only 15 minutes to spare. They entered the back of the house and hid in the basement. Smiz had already set up various boobie traps inside the house. He wanted the last hit to be hands on so he had to incapacitate them first.

Murder got into his Audi after donning his vest and loading his twin Mac-11's. Before he pulled out he just sat in the idling car smoking a Newport. He vowed that after he had gotten Milky back that he would kill every Wild Boy that was left breathing.

Flames and his team pulled into the block where the house stood. They circled the block twice before parking. They checked their equipment before getting out and then exited the truck. Flames sent one dude to the rear and he and the other good decided they would bum rush the front door. Once in place they moved in unison hitting both door at once.

Act II

Flames and the goon burst through the front door but before they could shoot a round they tumbled through a huge hole in the floor 50 feet in the basement. They landed on the concrete floor. Knocking themselves out. The goon at the backdoor never saw Raheem as he burst through the backdoor and before he could react, Raheem hit him in his forehead with two hollow tip rounds from his Smith and Wesson Glock 357. By the time the goon's body hit the floor Smiz was already standing over his prey in the basement. Raheem joined him seconds later.

"Get their guns and tie them up for me," said Smiz with a smirk.

"Aright then what?"

"Nothing. You can leave after that I'm going to torture them and slice them up piece by piece and then scatter their pieces all over the bottom of the Chesapeake Bay.

"You do know that you mentally disturbed and psychotic."

"Thank you for noticing, now leave me to my work, tell 40 I'll check in when I'm finished here."

"Will do Mister Sicko," joked Raheem as he left.

St. Louis put the still unconscious Milky in the backseat of the van and drove to Owings Mills with 40 following close behind. Murder pulled out in his Audi and made his way to Owings Mills also. He found it odd that he hadn't heard from anyone on his team so he dialed Flames cell phone only to be greeted by a strange voice telling him that his Boy wasn't able to take the call but, he would be dying to return the call. Then the voice began to laugh maniacally before hanging up.

St. Louis parked the van in the designated parking space and moved

Milky to the front seat still unconscious she began to stir so he taped her mouth and hands. He placed the duffel bag on the passenger seat, hit the door locks and closed the door. 40 sat in his vehicle at the other end of the parking lot and watched. Suddenly another ideal entered his mind and he knew it would be the perfect way to wrap up his plan.

40 rolled down the window and called a disheveled looking older lady over to the car.

"Excuse me Miss, would you like to make a quick hundred bucks?"

Murder was furious now! He was seeing red; the only thing on his mind now was finishing off the Wild Boyz and then leaving with Milky to start a new life. He was about 10 minutes away from the supposed drop, even though he never planned on dropping off any money.

The lady was still on the phone and standing at 40's window when St. Louis got into the car.

"Yes officer the minivan is black with tinted windows and there're some suspicious Black guys in it. It looks like a drug deal or something. Please Hurry! The lady hung up and 40 handed her a hundred dollar bill."

"You can keep the phone too," said 40.

"Thank you young man!" said the lady as she walked off and boarded the bus.

Murder turned into the parking lot 5 minutes later and caught sight of the minivan in the designated spot. He couldn't see through the tinted windows but, he knew that someone was inside awaiting the cash. He parked the Audi, got out and walked around the trunk. He looked around to make sure no one was staring before he pulled on a black mask and grabbed his twin Mac-11's from the trunk. He closed it and began to walk quickly toward the minivan. The only thing on his mind was making someone pay for what was going on, with that thought in his mind he opened fire on the driver side of the van emptying the clips of both Mac-11's.

Once both guns had finished raining hollow-tips on the driver side door, Murder slowly walked up to the van. He was determined to see the face of his enemy and to retrieve the paper with address on it. Once he arrived at the driver's door he looked into the shattered window. What he saw made his blood run cold.

"Oh My God No!! Please God No! Nooo!" screamed Murder.

He snatched opened the door, dropped both guns on the ground and began to sob.

Milky's bullet riddled body was slumped in the driver's seat. She had been struck by multiple bullets and there was little pieces of bone and flesh everywhere. Murder began to howl and his tears began to flow freely as he undid the tape on her hands and mouth. He was still cradling her dead corpse when the police surrounded him their weapons drawn.

40 and St. Louis watched the whole situation from beginning to end, and as Murder was being booked for the Murder of Milky they decided it was time to leave the scene.

As they were exiting the parking lot 40's phone rang...

"Yeah," said 40.

"The kid was released at the hospital in Downtown Richmond and I'm on 95 North returning as we speak," said Samir.

"Good, Go home, I'll call you in the morning!"

"What about Drew?"

"The lawyer said the charges were dropped, it was investigated and the police found no wrong doing. He still in the hospital though!"

"Aright Boss."

"One!"

"One!"

6 months later...

Murder was found guilty for the murder of Milkeena Steward and her unborn fetus. He was sentenced to life without parole.

Salty fled to North Carolina where he was robbed and killed by some Country boys he was tryna burn.

The Wild Boyz closed down all drug operations and 40 decided to leave Baltimore for Atlanta. Everyone else remained in Maryland and continued to deal with everyday life.

Lil Money was taken into Foster care in Virginia because his mother or father could not be found.

ABOUT THE AUTHOR

Dion Williams also known as D. Will was born on January 14, 1975 to John R. and Sheila J. Williams. Dion was raised in the City of Baltimore Maryland. He received both a public and a private school education before stint in the U.S. Army.

Through both book and street intelligence, Mr. Williams managed to navigate a host of pitfalls and accomplishments before deciding to pick up a pen and welcome you, the reader to the world created by both imagination and circumstances of the streets.